Myra
The Child of Adoption

A REPRINT OF THE CLASSIC BEADLE DIME NOVEL

Myra

The Child of Adoption

Romance of Real Life

BY MRS. ANN S. STEPHENS

With an Introduction by Chris Enss

TWODOT®

GUILFORD, CONNECTICUT
HELENA, MONTANA

AN IMPRINT OF THE GLOBE PEQUOT PRESS

A · T W O D O T® · B O O K

Myra, The Child of Adoption (Dime Novel No. 3) was previously published by Beadle and Company in 1860.

Text by Chris Enss © 2006 Morris Book Publishing, LLC

TwoDot is a registered trademark of Morris Book Publishing, LLC.

Text design: Lisa Reneson

Library of Congress Cataloging-in-Publication Data
Stephens, Ann S. (Ann Sophia), 1810–1886.
 Myra : the child of adoption : romance of real life / Ann S. Stephens ; with an introduction by Chris Enss.— Rev. ed.
  p. cm.
 ISBN-13: 978-0-7627-4082-6
 ISBN-10: 0-7627-4082-5
 1. Gaines, Myra Clark, 1805–1885—Fiction. I. Title.
 PS2919.S3M97 2006
 813'.3—dc22
                              2006007537

Manufactured in the United States of America
Revised Edition/First Printing

AN INTRODUCTION TO
BEADLE & ADAMS
DIME NOVELS

An extraordinary series of books was offered to the public in 1860. The editors at Beadle & Adams Publishing proudly presented reading material specifically geared to the female market. With few exceptions, dime novels authored by women centered on fearless females who braved the open prairie beyond the Mississippi, where they encountered outlaws, warring Indians, and wild animals and endured frigid temperatures, searing heat, and torrential downpours. These fictitious heroines faced desperate challenges bravely, but maintained their beauty and femininity. The combination of determined spirit and classic charm made these characters admirable. They also served as role models for young girls and women—in particular, those hoping to find a better life beyond the Rocky Mountains.

Some historians suggest government officials encouraged dime novel publishers because the books helped persuade settlers to travel to the New Frontier. The country was on the verge of a civil war, and western migration had slowed as a result of the impending conflict between the North and the South. During the war, the Union sought to encourage the continued expansion of the U.S. boundaries and used every means at their disposal to do so.

Politicians recognized women could bring social order to the uncivilized West. The quicker the West was tamed, the easier it would be to claim the territories and their riches to help fund the North's

*Advertisement for the first Beadle & Adams
dime novel as it appeared in the
New York Tribune, June 1860*

cause. Critics who believed that dime novels were being exploited to
further the North's cause felt the books were harmful because they
promoted an unrealistic idea of life in a rugged new land.

Beadle & Adams's reason for publishing the popular books was
mostly financial. Dime novels were the most popular form of literary
entertainment from 1860 to 1915. They were fast, exciting reads, and
their size made them easy to transport. Women in the East pored over
the material while doing their daily chores or on their lunch breaks.
Women on their way west read while on the stage or around the
campfire. Beadle & Adams novels focused on dramatic struggles and
hardships—often of the American pioneer. A strong sense of patriotism or morality was at the heart of each story.

Brothers Erastus and Irwin Beadle and entrepreneur Robert Adams weren't the first to publish such quick adventure novels—they merely issued the material in a continuous series instead of issuing them sporadically, and sold them at a fixed price of ten cents. The novels were printed on the least expensive, lowest-grade paper available. The type was small, no more than two or three columns. The trim size was 6⅝ by 4½ inches, and the books were generally 96 to 128 pages long. Each title was issued in a brightly colored wrapper with an illustration depicting the adventurous subject of the book in a dangerous setting.

As dime novels were not considered by the literary world to be on par with other books, the material was primarily relegated to being sold at newsstands and specialty shops. That restriction did not hinder sales, and the Beadle & Adams Publishing formula proved to be extremely profitable. From 1860 to 1872, the company dominated the cheap fiction market. Authors hoping to get their story read by the company's chief editors had to adhere to very specific submission guidelines.

So much is said, and justly, against a considerable number of papers and libraries now on the market, that we beg to repeat the following announcement and long standing instructions to all contributors:

Authors who write for our consideration will bear in mind that—

We prohibit subjects of characters that carry an immoral taint—

We prohibit the repetition of any occurrence which, though true, is yet better untold—

We prohibit what cannot be read with satisfaction by every right-minded person old and young alike—

We require your best work—

We require unquestioned originality—

We require pronounced strength of plot and high dramatic interest in story—

We require grace and precision of narrative and correctness of composition.

Authors must be familiar with characters and places which they introduce and not attempt to write in a field of which they have no intimate knowledge.

Those who fail to reach the standard here indicated cannot write acceptably for our several libraries, or for any of our publications.

The Beadle & Adams Editorial Staff – January 1861

Many talented writers contributed to the Beadle & Adams publications on their way to becoming literary giants. Ned Buntline, Mark Twain, and Louisa May Alcott were a few of the gifted authors who wrote for the publishing house.

With the exception of famous authors such as Charlotte Brontë, Alexandre Dumas, and Buffalo Bill Cody, the dime novel characters were better known than their creators. Hurricane Nell, the Queen of the Saddle; Lasso Bess, the Trapper; and Mountain Kate were daring women that readers couldn't get enough of. Their exploits and challenges were the topic of many fireside conversations.

At a time when job opportunities for women outside the home were limited, Beadle & Adams employed a number of female authors. Ann S. Stephens, Metta Victor, and Mrs. Henry J. Thomas were among the top moneymakers for the company. Not unlike the women they wrote about, these authors represented a pioneering spirit in the field of popular fiction. Their readership went beyond the western Plains into Europe. Ladies in France and England who enjoyed the romantic tales of the American West yearned to embark on the same quests as the women in the books.

Romance books penned by women were among the best-selling dime novels. As such, proposals on that topic were approved over other subject matter. Male writers in tune with the market submitted love stories under female pennames. Popular Beadle & Adams author Albert Aiken used the pseudonym Frances Helen Davenport, and author Frank S. Finn used the nom de plume Eve Lawless.

By 1891 the dime novel had been replaced by more serious types of literature. Educational books and children's stories had risen in popularity. At the turn of the twentieth century, the Beadle & Adams staff made significant changes in the layout and covers of their publications. They also lowered the price of the material to a nickel. Still, they could never recapture the success the bold, soft-bound novels once knew.

Original copies of Beadle & Adams dime novels are rare. According to historians at the California State Historical Library, if the books are found in a complete set of an author's work and in good condition, they could be worth more than $500.

The language used in these historic dime novels is a combination of Victorian-era English and a vocabulary indicative of the time. In an essay in the *Yale Review* in 1937, historian Merle Curti wrote of the dime novels that these "fragile, rare, and highly fugitive books will be useful ... to anyone interested in proletarian literature," and that they "must be taken in account particularly by those interested in the democratization of culture ... in the rise and reinforcement of our traditions and adventure and rugged individualism, in the development of class consciousness, and in the growth of American patriotism and nationalism."

It is with great pleasure we bring this classic series of Beadle & Adams dime novels to a new generation. We're sure you'll find these melodramatic tales both entertaining and inspiring. Although these books were written more than a century ago, their themes of American spirit and determination, of courage and bravery, of heroism and patriotism, and of friendship, love, and honor are timeless.

Mrs. Ann S. Stephens

DIME NOVELIST
ANN SOPHIA
WINTERBOTHAM STEPHENS

It is true! God help me, it is true; but I thought he was dead. It was night, and I was so terrified that the face was not clear. Oh! If it were only death that he brings instead of these bonds.

—Excerpt from *Sybil Chase; or, The Valley Ranche. A Tale of California Life,* a dime novel by Mrs. Ann Stephens, published in April 1861

Ann Sophia Winterbotham, one of Beadle & Adams's most renowned authors, holds the distinction of writing the very first dime novel, *Malaeska, The Indian Wife of the White Hunter,* published in 1860.

Born in Humphreysville, Connecticut, in 1813, Ann Sophia Winterbotham was educated at a girl's school in South Britain. Her father, John Winterbotham, a manufacturer of woolen goods, early on instilled in his daughter a love for literature. He often read aloud to her, and the captivating stories she heard ultimately inspired her to pursue a career as a writer.

In 1831 Ann met and married a man who shared her passion, Edward Stephens, a journalist and the publisher of a magazine in Portland. After the pair exchanged vows, Edward moved his bride to his home in Maine and hired her as the editor of the periodical. From 1831 to 1836, Ann contributed much of her own work—including poems, sketches, and historical tales—to the publication.

The Stephens family moved to New York in 1837, hoping that physicians there could help Edward in his struggle with poor health (perhaps tuberculosis). Ann supported her husband and two children by working as the editor of *The Ladies Companion* magazine. The popular magazine offered helpful tips and articles on and about women.

In 1842 publishers of a competing periodical persuaded Ann to work for them. She was named assistant editor of *Graham's Magazine*, a position she shared with fellow author Edgar Allen Poe. Poe insisted the title was given to Ann merely to increase readership with women, and that it carried no real responsibility. The personality clash eventually drove Ann to resign her post.

Ann's disappointing experience with *Graham's Magazine* had a positive outcome. Instead of working for another male-dominated publication, she decided to establish her own periodical. She founded *The Ladies World* magazine in 1843. The magazine was in print less than a year when the owners of *Peterson's Ladies Magazine* offered Ann a job as the publication's associate editor. Her relationship with the magazine, either as an editor or contributor, spanned more than forty years.

From 1850 to 1852, Ann and her family embarked on a long journey through Europe. During her travels she was able to spend time with Charles Dickens, an author who had served as a major inspiration for her work. She also met with Russian royalty and visited with the Pope.

When the family returned to the United States, Ann, Edward, and their children divided their time between their home in New York and their new house in Washington, D.C. While wintering in the nation's capital, Ann hosted teas and evening meals for President Franklin Pierce, the First Lady, and various other political figures, all of whom enjoyed her work.

Four years after returning from her momentous trip abroad, Ann founded yet another magazine. The first edition of *Mrs. Stephens Illustrated New Monthly* was offered to the public in July 1856. While maintaining her own publication, she worked as an editor on *Brother Jonathan*, a weekly paper founded by her husband.

In addition to keeping up with her duties on two periodicals and caring for two homes and her son and daughter, Ann found time to author three novels. Two of those novels—*Fashion & Famine, The Tradesman's Daughter*, and her most critically acclaimed work, *The Old Homestead*—were published in a three-year time span, from 1856 to 1859.

The Old Homestead was the story of Christian redemption, with a diminutive and plain heroine at its center. The book—which exposed the despicable treatment of the mentally ill, orphans, and those in prisons—earned high praise from other authors and was recognized as the first material of its kind to deal with such a delicate theme. The novel had numerous reprintings and was even adapted for the stage.

Ann's association with the publishing house of Beadle & Adams began in 1859. Having read one of Ann's pieces in *The Ladies Companion* magazine, editor Irwin Beadle approached the intrepid author about reprinting the story for a new publication he hoped to create, called "dime novels." Ann agreed and was paid $250 for the story. Thirty thousand copies of Ann's story, *Malaeska, The Indian Wife of the White Hunter*, were sold, introducing the world to the ten-cent novella. *Malaeska, The Indian Wife of the White Hunter*, Ann's tragic story of love and prejudice in the American West, sold several hundreds of thousands of copies and sparked the enormous popularity of dime novels.

Ann's *Myra, the Child of Adoption*, was the third consecutive dime novel offered by Beadle & Adams in 1860. The book was loosely based on the life of a great New Orleans heiress who had been orphaned and spent years fighting the courts to regain her fortune. Female readers enjoyed the tale of the young woman who falls in love with the man who helped reclaim her heritage.

Though Ann's large following of fans craved her next dime novel, she was not content to focus solely on that form of writing. Between dime novels, she wrote books on crocheting, needlework, the Civil War, and subjects of her own personal interests and political ideals. Her book *A Pictorial History of the War for the Union* was published in 1865. The two-volume set outlined her position against slavery and described how she and others in a group she organized managed to ration their supplies to help support the North.

Ann expanded on her feelings about the Civil War in a series of articles entitled *High Life in New York*. Published under the pseudonym Jonathan Slide, the articles focused on an imaginary Yankee soldier's efforts to defend his country.

Ann Stephens wrote a total of eight dime novels for Beadle & Adams, including: *Malaeska, The Indian Wife of the White Hunter* (1860); *Sybil Chase; or, The Valley Ranche. A Tale of California Life* (1861); *Esther. A Story of the Oregon Trail* (1862); *Kirk, the Guide; or The Oregon Trail* (1862); *Ahmo's Plot; or The Governor's Indian Child* (1863); *Mahaska, The Indian Princess* (1863); and *The Indian Queen* (1864).

She died in Newport, Rhode Island, in August 1886. At the time of her death she was at the home of her publisher, working on her twenty-fourth full-length book.

CHAPTER ONE

MYRA, THE CHILD OF ADOPTION

One look upon thy face ere thou depart!
My daughter! it is soon to let thee go!
My daughter! with thy birth has gushed a spring
I knew not of—filling my heart with tears,
And turning with strange tenderness to thee—
A love, O God! it seems so—that must flow
Far as thou fleest, and wrap my soul and thee.
Henceforth thy love must be a yearning charm
Drawing me after thee. And so farewell!
                                        —Willis

The windows were all open, but shaded fold after fold with muslin transparent as dew drops, and snowy as the drifts of a summer cloud. The floor was spread with East India matting, and in a corner of a chamber stood a couch shaded with clouds of delicate lace and clad in snow white even to the floor. A great easy chair, covered with chaste dimity, stood close by the bed, and further off a miniature couch, snow-white also, save where the soft rose tints of an inner curtain, light and silken broke through the waves of snowy gossamer that flowed over it. Upon the pillow of this pretty couch lay a bouquet of flowers tied

1

loosely by an azure-colored ribbon, and more beautiful still a sleeping infant, with one tiny hand resting like a torn peach blossom, on its little bosom and its sweet lips parted smilingly, as a bud uncloses to the warm sunbeam. There, in its snowy nest, with the fragrant flowers sending their breath in and out through the misty draperies, and half smothered in delicate lace, lay the beautiful infant; and a little way off, upon the larger couch reposed another being in the first bud and bloom of womanly beauty, not asleep but with her large eyes wandering tenderly toward the infant, and from that to a bouquet of orange-blossoms and moss-roses that, feebly clasped in her delicate fingers, was yet falling apart and dropping its blossoms over the counterpane.

An air of gentle languor lay upon this young creature, and there was something more than that affectionate tenderness with which a mother regards her young child, in the look that she, from time to time, cast upon the slumbering infant—a shade of sadness, that but for her feeble state might have taken the strength of passionate regret, seemed ready to break from her eyes in a flood of tears whenever they dwelt longer than usual upon the babe. But when her grief was ready to break forth, she would allow her eyes to droop toward the flowers that seemed to have some pleasant association connected with their fragrance, and a sweet smile—not the less sweet that there was sadness in it—would part her lips while a faint sigh floated through them.

All at once the infant began to nestle in its crib, and opening its large brown eyes, turned them upon the recumbent female. As if her tears lay so near the surface as to require only this motion to set them flowing, the young mother, as she encountered the infantile glance, shuddered faintly, and large drops gathered in her eyes and fell one by one over her full but pale cheeks.

"I must not look at it, I must not learn to love it so," she murmured, turning her head away, and shading her tearful eyes with one hand. "Ah! why should I, a mother so young, and with a husband like *him*, always find every feeling, every impulse shackled as it springs from my heart? Why was there no one to shield my youth from the blight, that I feel, too surely, will cling around me to the end?"

The infant began to cry, and there came into the room a colored woman, tall and with that superb luxuriance of form that so frequently characterizes the dusky-hued woman of the South. She approached the crib and took the child in her arms, hushing it with a sort of cajoling attempt at tenderness that seemed to annoy the young mother not a little.

"Give the babe to me!" she said, feebly reaching forth her arms.

"Better not, better not, missus," replied the woman, pressing her full lips upon the velvet cheek resting on her bosom—a most unnatural pillow, as the unhappy mother felt all too keenly. "Nurse said last night that young missus must be kept quiet, and the baby not left to fret her so much."

"Fret me! my child fret me! Give it to me, I say," cried the young mother so passionately that the color broke over her pale cheek, like the abrupt opening of a rose-bud. "It is cruel, it is unkind, thus to keep a babe from its mother's bosom. He never ordered it. I know well enough it is not his wish that I should be tortured in this manner."

"Take the child to its mother. Why do you hesitate in obeying your mistress?" cried a firm and manly voice from the door; and with his lofty step somewhat subdued, a gentleman entered the chamber, whose air of authority awed the negress at once. He approached the young female, who had started eagerly up from her pillow, with every manifestation of deep tenderness in her voice and manner.

"Have you been waiting for me, Zulima?" he said, bending down to kiss the fair forehead of his wife. "I was kept longer than usual at the counting-house this morning."

"Oh! I knew that you would be here soon," replied the young wife, taking his hand between both hers, kissing it with a degree of passionate tenderness that thrilled through her feeble frame, till, in her weak state, excess of feeling became almost painful.

"What! because I scattered my path to your bedside with the flowers you have been wasting?" was the smiling reply.

"They were welcome and very sweet, for they told me that you were soon to follow," said the young wife, gathering the scattered flowers together with her hand. "See! your little daughter has kept hers in better condition. She is not old enough to tear her flowers to pieces the moment they come within reach!"

"Like her mother, ha! Zulima!" said the gentleman, shaking his head but smiling fondly all the time. "She must have more patience and less pride than her mother, this pretty child—or she will be—"

"As unfortunate and as unhappy as her mother has been" said the young wife, and her eyes filled with tears.

"I only hope she will be as lovely and as innocent, whatever her lot may prove, and as truly beloved, Zulima," he added, after a moment's pause; and with an expression of deep feeling mingled with a shade of sadness, the proud husband gazed upon his wife and child till the tears clouded his own fine eyes.

For a moment there was silence between the husband and wife. Both were gazing upon the infant, and both were occupied with thoughts where pain and tenderness were almost equally blended. Pride, stern and lofty pride, tinged the sweet current of his reflections, and she—impulsive young creature—thought of nothing but her sufferings, her passionate love for him, and of the beautiful child she was sheltering upon her bosom with one fairy arm, from which she had impatiently flung back the loose sleeve of her night-dress, as if detesting the delicate lawn for coming between her and that little form.

"You will not send her away!" said the young creature, lifting her eyes to the face of her husband, which was becoming more and more thoughtful each moment. "Ah' if you knew how much I love her!"

"I know—I know, Zulima," said the husband, interrupting the beautiful pleader with an accent which, though not unkind, told how the slightest opposition chafed his proud nature. "It is natural. You must love the child; who could help it? But do you not love me better? Do you not love its future fame?—its father's fame?—your own reputation, well enough to relinquish her for a time?"

4

"I have thought of it all—I know what the world will say of me—but I cannot give her up; indeed, indeed I cannot." The young mother rose in the bed, and with her child folded to her bosom with one arm, cast the other round the proud man's neck, and drew his face down till it touched the infant, as she covered his forehead with kisses. "You will keep us both; you will not take our child from me!"

"Zulima, it must be," said the husband, drawing gently back, and freeing himself from her fond embrace, while his fine features bespoke the terrible pain which it cost him to be firm. "While the man who has once claimed you for his wife remains unpunished, I cannot acknowledge you mine, legally, innocently mine, as in the sight of Heaven you are."

"I do not ask it. Let the world think of me as it likes. I will submit to reproach—to suspicion—anything. But leave my child—never."

"Zulima!" was the firm and almost reproachful reply, "do you think that your reputation is separate from mine? Shall I cast a stain upon my wife which no after time can efface, and then produce her, wronged and sullied, to society? Listen to me, Zulima; cease weeping and listen! The man is yet alive who has called you wife—"

"I know—I know!" cried the poor young creature, shuddering from head to foot, and burying her face in the pillows. "Oh say no more! I will give up my child—but spare me that subject!"

"No, Zulima. Let us speak of it this once, and then it shall be banished our lips forever. Think you that it is not painful to me as to you?"

"How painful it was might be guessed by the colorless cheeks and the quivering of that proud man's lips while he was speaking.

"While a mere child you became the dupe and victim of this vile man, De Grainges. He wronged your confidence, wronged your love—"

"No! no! I did not love him—I was a child; I knew not what love was!" broke in passionate murmurs from the pillow where Zulima's face was buried. "Do not say I loved that man!"

"My poor wife! I know that you did not love him. I know quite as well that you do love me. Look up, sweet child! I would give worlds that I could speak of all this without distressing you thus. Bear with me only a minute longer. My only wish is to reconcile you, if possible, to the inevitable."

"I will listen," replied the tortured young mother.

"I know, Zulima, that you were deceived by this bad man, that he wedded you while his wife was living, and that you fled from his home the moment this truth was made known. Of all this I was thoroughly convinced before you became my wife, but until this man is convicted in open court and before the whole world, how can I convince society of that which to me is a sacred truth? How, before the fact of his previous marriage is thus publicly substantiated, can I proclaim the union which has made me more than happy? Zulima, I am a proud man—sensitive to public opinion—careful of my standing in the world. Were a breath of suspicion to rest upon the fame of my wife, I should never be happy again. You are young—supposed to be unmarried—living here under the roof of my dearest friend, who, with one exception, is alone in my confidence. In a few months this man, now in prison, will receive the punishment of his crime. Do you not see the peril of keeping this child with you till after that event enables me to claim my wife before the world? Zulima! look up—say that you forgive me the pain I am causing. Say that, for my sake, you will submit to have this little one sent from you for a season—only for a season."

Subdued and touched to the heart by the depth of feeling with which this appeal was made, Zulima arose from the pillow where she had been striving to subdue her grief, and taking the infant in her trembling arms, motioned her husband to receive it. The moment she was relieved from the sweet burden, the young creature fell back, and closing her eyes, tried to check the grief that, however suppressed, still clamored at her heart. It was all in vain: The tears gushed like shattered diamonds though the thick and silky lashes, and she grasped the counterpane nervously with one hand, in a terrible strife to force back the agony that was choking her. Poor young mother! She felt with that keen intuition like a prophecy that she was not parting from her child for a season but forever.

"You consent, Zulima? You will give up our little one with no anger, and without all this bitter grief?" cried the strong man, pale as death, and bending over the young mother with the child pressed to his bosom.

"I will, I do," burst from those pale and trembling lips.

The husband turned away; his limbs trembled, his eyes were blinded with moisture, and the weight of that little babe seemed to bend and sway his strong frame, as if he had been a reed. He looked back upon the mother. There she lay, the wet eyelids closed and quivering, her white lips pressed together, and so pale, that but for the agitation of her features she might have seemed stricken dead in the midst of her anguish. He returned to the couch.

"Zulima, would you kiss the babe before it goes!"

"I dare not—I dare not," broke from those pale lips. Then Zulima held back her sobs, for his footsteps were departing—a door closed—husband and child both were gone. Then the mother's anguish broke forth, her arms were flung upward, her quivering hands clasped wildly together—a moment and they fell heavily upon the orange flowers that still littered the bed, crushing them in her utter insensibility.

Then, while the young wife lay so pale and deathly there stole toward the bed that negro woman, who bent down till the bright Madras 'kerchief turbaning her forehead mingled with the chestnut tresses that lay scattered over the shoulder and bosom of the sufferer. She listened a moment, as if to make herself quite certain that what seemed so deathly was not death itself, and then glided from the chamber.

The negress stole softly through the open hall and into a spacious garden; a row of small, white buildings stood at the farther extremity, gleaming in snowy patches through the vines and trees that embowered that portion of the garden. These were the slave dwellings

7

belonging to a rich plantation some three miles from New Orleans—belonging to the husband of Zulima, and occupied for a season by his bosom friend that the infancy of his child might be honorably sheltered. And here in a little whitewashed room of the slave dwelling this bosom friend was impatiently watching the approach of the female slave whom he had placed—a dark spy—in the bed-chamber of that helpless young wife. With his face close to one of the four panes of glass that admitted light to the humble room, he watched the fiery colors of the Madras turban, which the woman always wore, as it glided like some gorgeous bird through the thick foliage, nearer and nearer to the den where he had for two hours been waiting for news from the sick-chamber. The slave entered her dwelling and sat down before her master, full of that consequential assumption that a little power is certain to call forth in one of her ignorant and degraded class.

"Well, Louisa," said the master, with a show of careless indifference, for he was of a cool and subtle temperament, with passions slow and calculating, but all the more grasping for the deliberation, which, like well-trained hounds, they were let free from the leash of his strong will. "Well, Louisa, how is the lady this morning?"

"Oh, she am about de same, Massa Ross—no danger of her going off dis bout anyhow," replied the negress, turning her head on one side and moving a palm-leaf fan before her face with an air of self-conceit that made her auditor smile, spite of his preoccupation.

"She just had a little fainting spell when I come out, but it won't last long—no danger!"

"Has she had any visitors this morning; has *he* been there, Louisa?"

"Dar, now, you ask me dat, Mass Ross, just as if he didn't come ebery morning of him life."

"Then he has been there," rejoined the man, "and left her fainting. Tell me, Louise—oh here is the Napoleon that I promised."

"There, that am something like Massa Ross," and the negress tied the gold in a corner of her handkerchief, and thrust it into her bosom. "Yes, he was there a long time."

"Well," interrupted Ross, evidently getting impatient, "tell me all that passed, word for word; do not forget a look or a syllable—and another gold piece is ready when you have done."

And the negress, thus stimulated, told him all. That scene of tender anguish—the struggle of love and pride which she had witnessed in the sick chamber—all was related; and oh! how its exquisite pathos, its touching dignity was desecrated by the vulgar mind and coarse speech of that slave woman!

Ross listened to it all, his face changing with every sentence; for, with only that coarse witness, he did not think it necessary to control his features with the dissimulation that had become a habit. He listened, and as he felt, thus the evil man looked. When the woman ceased speaking, the exultation of a fiend was in the smile that curled his lip.

"And he was determined—spite of her caresses, spite of her tears. I knew it would be so. He is not a man to waver, having once taken a resolution—but the child, Louise? I have recommended a woman up the river to take charge of it, but you, my good Louisa, must still be its nurse. It seems a feeble little thing; do you not think so, Louisa?"

"Feeble! Lor a massa! No, it's the best-natured, healthy little thing I ever see," was the reply, and Louisa agitated her palm-leaf fan with considerable violence.

"But away from you, Louisa, with someone less kind, it may become sickly in a very little time you know."

"Sure enough!" and Louisa half suspended the action of her fan, as she fell into a fit of profound contemplation.

"With you to give it medicine and superintend, if it were ill, I should feel quite safe," said Ross, and a strange, fiendish smile crept over his lips. "Of course, I should come and see you very often."

"Oh! you would. Well, den, I haven't nothing to say against going with the baby."

"Wherever I send you, Louisa?"

"Well, yes, I don't care, if it isn't so far off that you can't come once a week or so to see us, Massa Ross; but I won't go far, now I tell you."

"Well, now, go to your charge. I will see you again tomorrow."

The negress arose, and with an insolent twist of her head to the left shoulder, stood in the doorway fanning herself.

"Well," said, Ross, impatiently, "well, what are you waiting for now!"

"Dis piece of gold in my bosom, Massa Ross," and the negress placed a plump ebony hand upon her heart. "It is 'gun beginning to feel lonesome."

"Oh! I had forgotten; here, here."

Louisa drew forth the pocket handkerchief, which, from its embroidery and exquisite lace, must have been purloined from her mistress, and a second Napoleon was nested in her bosom.

"Stop," said Ross, as she was going out; "you said that the lady was fainting—that *he* took the child forth in his arms. Where is it now?"

"How should I know? I s'pose he took the baby to your wife. She was in the back parlor, and he turned that way."

"There he is now. Go back into the room, Louisa, go back!" Ross seized his hat as he spoke, and leaving the slave house wound through a grove of fruit trees that sheltered him from sight, and taking a serpentine path came leisurely forth into that part of the garden where he had seen Mr. Clark. The proud man was walking hurriedly forward, his arms folded and one white aristocratic hand thrust into the bosom of his black dress. He was very pale, and his finely cut features bore traces of great internal anguish. He saw Ross, and turned quickly toward him.

"It is over, my friend; it is all over," he said, grasping the hand which Ross extended and wringing it hard. A smile, full of proud anguish, broke the firm and classical beauty of his mouth, and his eyes spoke volumes of suffering.

"What is over? What has happened?" inquired Ross, startled and turning almost as white as his friend.

"My wife! my child!"

"What of them? What has happened to them, my friend?"

"Nothing but that which was inevitable. But Zulima, my poor, poor wife! It would wring your heart to see how she suffers from the separation from her child."

"But the child; is it yet with her?"

"Hark!" said the other, lifting his hand. "Do you not hear?"

It was the sound of a carriage driving rapidly from the house. Mr. Clark seemed listening to the sound as if his life was departing with it—fainter and fainter from his bosom. There was something in his countenance which Ross dared not disturb, though his soul was burning with curiosity to know why the common sound of carriage-wheels grinding through the gravelly soil should so profoundly agitate his benefactor. The sound grew distant, and died away before another word was spoken, then Mr. Clark turned toward his false friend, his nerves hitherto drawn to their most rigid tension relaxed, and his eye met the gaze with which Ross was curiously regarding him with an appeal for sympathy that would have touched a heart for stone.

"It is gone!" he said, in a broken voice. "My child is gone!"

"Your child gone? when, where?" cried Ross, fearfully excited. "Surely you have not sent the infant from its mother so abruptly—and—and without consulting—I mean without informing your best friend."

"That carriage—you heard it—bore away Zulima's child!" said the unhappy father, mournfully.

"But where has it gone? With whom is it placed?"

"It is placed with one whom I have long known, the noble and childless wife of an old and dear friend. Myra will be to them as their own child, till I claim her again."

"And may I not know the people, and the place?" inquired the false friend. "The child of my benefactor is dear to me as my own."

"I have pledged myself to secrecy in this. It was the desire of my friend," repeated Mr. Clark, "but for that you should know everything. All this concealment will soon be over; a few weeks and this man must be sentenced. Then wife and child shall take possession of their home before the world. In this you can help me. I cannot well appear in person to press forward this man's conviction, but you, my friend, will use every effort to relieve me from this painful position. My poor wife scarcely suffers more than I do."

"I will do everything that you desire. Indeed, the commonest gratitude should ensure that," said Ross, pressing his patron's hand, but with restless and nervous haste in his manner. "Shall I set out for the city at once?"

"No, no, seek your wife first; tell her to comfort my poor Zulima. I cannot see her now; without wishing to reproach me, she could not help it. I tell you, Ross, I would rather encounter a squadron of armed men than the look of those soft eyes as they followed her child this morning when I took it from her. It was the glance of a wounded fawn, as we have often seen it, turned upon the hunter."

"I will see my wife at once," replied Ross, unable with all his duplicity to conquer the disappointment that was consuming him. "Then I will depart for the city, and make a strong effort to bring De Grainges to his trial."

"It is strange," said Mr. Clark, "but some influence that I can not fathom seems to keep back this man's sentence. The court, as if it were trifling with his case only to perpetuate my troubles, keeps putting off his sentence from day to day with cruel pertinacity. But now I am resolved that it shall be more prompt; this hidden influence must and shall be revealed."

Ross listened to the first portion of this speech with a cold and crafty smile playing and deepening about his mouth, but at the close this smile died away, and with it every vestige of color—his eyes wandered rapidly from object to object, avoiding the face of his benefactor, and when Mr. Clark would have spoken again, he forgot all the habitual deference of his manner and interrupted him.

"Have no trouble about this man, De Grainges; I will attend to him at once. The cause of this unaccountable delay in the court shall be ascertained and remedied. Now that I see how deeply your happiness is involved, no effort shall be wanting on my part to bring the trial to an issue. To this end, I must start for the city at once."

Ross held out his hand, and grasped that of his patron.

"Accomplish this for me, Ross, and no being ever lived more grateful than I shall be," said the generous man. "I depend on you."

"You may, most positively," was the emphatic reply; and wringing the hand he held, Ross left the garden. He met a servant in the hall, and accosted him with the sharp command to have a horse saddled. Then, passing into the inner room, he spoke a few hasty words, not to his wife but to the black woman, Louisa, and then hurried to the stable.

With the sluggish habits of his race, the negro was lazily dragging forth a saddle from its repository when his master came up booted and with a riding whip in his hand.

"Walk quick, you scoundrel!" he said, laying the whip over the sleek negro with a force that made the old fellow start into something resembling haste; but even this unheard of activity did not satisfy the master; he snatched the saddle, flung it over the horse, and set his teeth firmly together, as he buckled the girth. Sharply ordering the man out of his way, he sprang upon the horse and dashed toward the city, at first in a light canter; but the moment he was out of sight, the high-spirited animal was put to the top of his speed and horse and man flew like lightning along the road.

At each turn of the road, Ross would lean forward on his saddle and take a new survey of the distance, muttering his disappointment in half-gasped sentences, as he sped along.

"Oh, if I could but overtake the carriage before it reaches the city! A single glimpse of it might be enough—nothing should take me from the track; nothing, nothing. Ha! that is it—no, only a sugar-cart.

Why did I let him keep me? I must, I will know who these people are—no, no, I am foiled at last!"

This exclamation was followed by a sharp check to the horse, who was still bounding forward at the top of his speed. The city lay before him; but along the winding highway, over which his eye ran like lightning, there was no carriage at all resembling the one that Louisa had described to him as that which had borne her young charge away.

At a slow pace, but with his horse reeking with the effects of his former hot speed, Ross rode into the city. He took a circuitous route, to his own counting-house, and held a long consultation with a young man whom he found there. This lasted several hours; and then the two walked arm-in-arm toward the city prison.

Through the gloomy labyrinths of this prison the two men made their way, conversing together in low voices; a turnkey went before them, humming a tune to himself, and sometimes raising an accompaniment by playfully dashing a huge iron key, which he held in one hand, against the door of some prisoner's cell, smiling grimly as he heard the poor inmate spring forward, in the vain hope that some friend had come to break the gloom of his bondage. From time to time, the two visitors seemed to study this man's face with close scrutiny; and as some new manifestation of character broke forth in his manner or his song, they would exchange glances that were full of meaning.

"Offer him gold!" whispered Ross to his companion. "Say that is for his trouble; we can judge something by the manner in which he receives it."

"True," was the emphatic but whispered reply, "it will be a sure test."

The officer paused at the entrance of a cell, and placed his key in the lock. "This is De Grainges' cell, gentlemen; how long will you wish to stay with him?"

"We may wish to remain so long that you will suffer some inconvenience," said Ross's companion, dropping his hand into a pocket with that easy grace which renders the most singular acts of some men perfectly natural in their seeming. "Here is something to repay the trouble we may occasion."

The turnkey reached forth his hand eagerly for the silver coin which he supposed the stranger was about to offer him, but when he saw a bright piece of gold glittering in his palm, the sudden joy of his heart broke with a sort of gloating ferocity over his face, and with a low chuckle he folded his other hand over the gold and began to rub the palms together with the coin between them in a warm clasp, as if he thought thus to infuse some portion of the precious metal into his own person.

Ross and his companion had stepped within the cell, and thus, clouded with semi-darkness themselves, watched the man, whose face was fully revealed in the broadly lighted corridor.

"It will do," whispered Ross, smiling, "it will do."

"Yes," said the other thoughtfully, "he is one of those who would sell his soul for money."

The man said this with the air of one who reflected sadly upon the infirmities of human nature, and really felt shocked at the gross cupidity that himself had tempted; and so it was. He did not reflect that he himself was there for no purpose on earth but to barter *his own* soul for the very yellow dross, only in a larger amount; that he was ready to yield to this man's bartered treachery; that all the difference between himself and the man he tempted lay in the price which each set upon his integrity. But the great villain despised the lesser sincerely, and sighed that human nature could be so degraded. So it is all over the world. Those who shroud their crimes in purple and fine linen ever do and ever will look down with benign contempt on those who fold lesser crimes scantily in poverty and rags, so scantily that the world sees them as they are: coarse, rude, and glaring.

Thus, shaking their heads and sighing over the degeneracy of the human heart, these two arch-villains entered the cell of De Grainges, the bigamist, leaving the officer without to gloat over his piece of gold.

A tall man, pale from confinement and yet possessed of a certain air of languid elegance, sat within the cell writing. He looked up as the two visitors entered and regarded them with an expression of nervous surprise, but observing that they were gentlemen in appearance, arose courteously, and placed the chair, in which he had been sitting, for Ross. The cell contained but two seats, and the prisoner stood up with his arms folded, and leaning against the wall in a position that had much grace in it.

"You have come, gentlemen," said the prisoner, in a low, sad voice, "you have doubtless come to tell me that the time of my sentence has arrived?"

"No," said Ross, "that would be a painful task, and one from which we are happily saved. We come, as friends, to ask some questions regarding this singular case. Perhaps we may have the power—we certainly have the will—to serve you."

"It is too late," replied the prisoner, sadly. "My trial is over. Why they have not sentenced me before this is incomprehensible."

"To you, perhaps, but not to us. You have strong friends outside; those who have done something in keeping back the sentence, and may do more—obtain, for instance, a new trial."

"To what end?" questioned the prisoner. "I am guilty. I have confessed it. In the wild delirium of a passion that was never equaled in the heart of man, I married the most confiding and lovely creature that ever lived. The fraud was detected. My wife—my living wife forced herself into the home where I had sheltered my falsely-won bride. Zulima would not love the villain who had wronged her. She left me; and without her I care very little whether it is to a prison or a grave."

"But what if Zulima loved you yet? What if she only desired that in this trial your right to her could be established?"

The prisoner shook his head.

"I only say," continued Ross, "if this were the case; if a new trial were granted, if there was no lack of funds to pave the way through court, would you not, having a new trial, suppress the proofs of this former marriage? Might not your wife herself be persuaded to aid in clearing you?"

"No," replied the prisoner, firmly. "It could not be. My wife pursues me with that strong hate which is born of baffled passion. Zulima ceased to love me."

"Because she believed her marriage unlawful," said Ross.

"It was unlawful. I have acknowledged it again and again. Zulima had nothing left—nothing but her freedom from the man that had wronged her to hope for. I would not deprive her of that."

"And if the means were before you? If you could obtain a new trial, this first marriage, you are certain, would be proven against you?"

"I am very certain," replied the prisoner.

"Remember, if they fail to prove the first marriage, you are free forever, and Zulima is your lawful wife. Is not this worth an effort?"

The unhappy man clasped his hands, and for a moment there broke through his sad eyes a luster that was perfectly dazzling.

"Worth an effort!" he said. "Oh, heavens! I would die but to see her look upon me again with love for a single moment."

"Then why not make the effort?"

"Because I know that Zulima has ceased to love me. She is young, beautiful. I feel that she has brought me here not for revenge but that herself may attain honorable freedom. I would not raise my hand to thwart her in the just object."

The two men looked anxiously at each other. They were astounded by the strange magnanimity of the prisoner.

"I tell you," said Ross, earnestly, "this thing can be brought about. Your counsel have seen the witnesses. Gold is a potent agent. Even your wife yields; she will not appear. You can be cleared of this charge: You can claim Zulima as your lawful wife. We pledge ourselves to accomplish all that we have proposed."

"Gentlemen, you seem kind, and I thank you. But I know that the wrong which I inflicted on that young girl has been followed by her aversion; she has told me so. She is not my lawful wife; without her

17

love—her firm, earnest love, I would not claim her if she were. All that she desires is freedom; that she shall have, though it cost my life instead of a few years' imprisonment."

Ross arose and went into the corridor, where he conversed in a low voice and very earnestly with the turnkey. Meantime the prisoner sat down in the empty chair and, burying his face in his hands, seemed to be lost in bitter thought. When Ross returned he arose and stood up, but his face was haggard, and he seemed to suffer much from the struggle that had been aroused in his breast.

"Then you are determined not to claim a new trial?"

"I am," was the reply.

"Perhaps it is as well; but we are the friends of Zulima. She suffers; she shrinks from the thought of your imprisonment. This new appeal may be impossible, but there is another way. Your trial has done all for Zulima that can be accomplished; it sets her free. Now she would give that to you which your self devotion will secure to her—freedom. Tonight, De Grainges, the means of escape will be provided; at day-break, tomorrow, a vessel sails for Europe; you must become one of her passengers."

"And does *she* desire this?" asked the prisoner, aroused all at once from the stubborn resolve of self-sacrifice that had possessed him.

"She does; we are her messengers."

"Tonight—this is sudden! and she desires it? She deems the trial that has taken place sufficient for her emancipation from the hateful bonds that made her mine. You are certain of this?"

"Most certain."

"And the means of escape?"

"Leave that to us. The time, midnight; be ready. That is all we desire of you."

"I will be ready," said the young man, falling into the chair which Ross had just left, and overcome with a sudden sense of freedom—freedom given by the woman whom he had so deeply wronged. His nerves, hitherto so firm, began to tremble, and covering his face with both hands, he burst into tears. When he looked up the two strangers had left the cell.

The next morning, when Ross entered his counting-room, he found the turnkey talking with his partner. Just then Mr. Clark entered also, but with a harassed and anxious expression of countenance.

"My friend," said Ross, advancing toward him, "you have come at the right moment to hear this man's news from his own lips. I fear it will give you pain. No, I had better tell it myself; he is a stranger, and knows nothing of your interest in the mother. Step this way, sir."

"What is this? For what would you prepare me? Zulima—"

"Is well, and becoming reconciled to her loss; but De Grainges—"

"What of him, sir? what of that unhappy man?" inquired Mr. Clark, sternly.

"He has broken prison; he escaped last night."

Mr. Clark staggered. The color left his lip, and he leaned heavily on the back of a chair. "My poor, poor wife! Will her trials never have an end?" he exclaimed with deep feeling, and turning hastily he left the counting-room.

"It will be some time before he acknowledges her now," said Ross, in a low voice, to his partner. "See how his step wavers."

"That may waver, but his pride never will," was the low reply.

"Never!" said Campbell.

And he was right. Poor, poor Zulima!

CHAPTER TWO

POOR, POOR ZULIMA!

Trifles, light as air,
Are, to the jealous, confirmations strong
As proofs of holy writ.
                    —Othello

It was spring-time in the South—that rich, bright season more luxurious in foliage and profuse in fragrance than our warm and mellow summers ever are. The orange-trees were all in flower; carnations blushed warm and glowing upon the garden banks; the grass was mottled with tiny blossoms, gorgeous and sweet as the air they breathed. All around the house that Zulima occupied was hedged in with honey-suckles and prairie-roses, that sheltered the grounds and leaped up here and there among the magnolia-trees, lacing them together in festoons and arcades of fantastic beauty.

Poor, poor Zulima! With this beautiful paradise to wander in, with the sweet air, the warm sky, and all that world of flowers, how unhappy she was! Alone—utterly alone!—her child slept in the bosom of another; her husband had been months away in the far North; an unacknowledged wife, a bereaved parent, how could she choose but weep? Weeks had gone by and no letter reached her. At first her husband had written every day; and with his letters, eloquent of love, lying against her heart, she could not be wholly miserable. Thinking of him she sometimes forgot to mourn for her child. At first she had been greatly distressed by the impediments which the flight of De Grainges had multiplied against the acknowledgment of her marriage, but this event had in no degree shaken the holy trust which that young heart placed in the object of its love. Singularly unambitious in her desires but impetuous in feeling, she felt only the continued secrecy maintained regarding her marriage, because it separated her from the babe she had learned to love so intensely. True, it served as a restraint upon her husband and frequently deprived her of his presence, but with her imaginative nature, the slight romance of this privacy only served to keep her affections more vivid and her fancy more restless. She was all impulse, all feeling, and sometimes, like a caged bird, she grew wild and restive under the restraints that necessity had placed upon her.

Weeks went by, one after another, and now Zulima grew wild with vague fears. Why was he silent? Where could he be wandering thus to forget her so completely? Her nights were sleepless; her eyes grew bright and wild with feverish anxiety. That young heart was in every way prepared for the poison that was to be poured into it drop by drop, till jealousy, that most fierce and bitter of all the passions, should break forth in its might and change her whole being.

Zulima had gone forth alone, not into the garden to sigh among its wilderness of blossoms, but away, with an aching heart and pale forehead, to suffer among the wild nooks of the neighboring hollows. Here nature started to life in harsher beauty, and sent forth her sweets with a sort of rude waywardness, forming a contrast to the voluptuous air and over cultivation that closed in her home, as it were, from the rough and true things of the world.

Another day was to be passed in that agony of impatience that none but those of a highly imaginative nature can ever dream of—a weary night had been spent, the morning had come—surely, surely that day *must* bring a letter from the absent one.

The air of her chamber—that chamber where her child had slept in her bosom, where *he* had been so often—she would not wait there; all the associations were so vivid, they goaded her on to keener impatience. She could not draw a deep breath in that room, thinking of *him* and *it*.

So, as I have said, Zulima stole forth and wandered away where all was wild as her own feelings, and a thousand times more tranquil. Ross had promised her to return very early from the city that day, when he hoped—the villain could not look into her eyes as he said it—when he hoped to bring a letter that would make his sweet guest smile again.

Zulima knew a place near the highway that led to the city—and yet sheltered from any traveler that might pass—by the broken banks of a rivulet. Thick trees fell over it, and in some places the water was completely embowered by the branches. She could hear the tread of a horse from the spot, should one pass up from the city; and so, with a cheek that kindled and a heart that leaped to each sound, the young creature sat down to wait. To wait! oh, how hard a task for her untamed spirit, her eager wishes! Never till her marriage with Mr. Clark had Zulima's vivid nature been fully aroused; never before had she been capable of the exquisite joy, the intense suffering that marked every stage of her attachment to that lofty and singular man. As she sat then by the lonely brook, the young creature gave herself up to a reverie that embraced all her life, for life with her seemed to have commenced only since she had met him. She drew forth his letters and read them again and again; tears blinded her sometimes, but she swept them away with her fingers and read on, kissing here and there a line that spoke most eloquently to her heart. She came to the last letter: That was more ardent in its language, and warmer in its expression of love, than any of the others had been. Why was this the last? What had happened to check a pen so eloquent, to chill a heart so warm? Was he dead? This was Zulima's thought; she never doubted his faith or distrusted his honor for a single moment. When the serpent jealousy reaches a heart like hers, it comes with a fling, striking his fang suddenly and at once. Zulima was not jealous, but that fierce pain lay coiled close by her heart, ready to make a leap that should envenom her whole being. More than once Zulima had started from her seat at some slight sound, which proved to be only a bird rising from the overhanging bank, or a rabbit leaping across the thick sward; and thus, between hope and despondency, dreams and thoughts of the stern real, the time crept by till noon. A wooden bridge scarcely lifted above the water, spanned the brook only a few yards from where Zulima was sitting. Here the bank fell abruptly, giving descent to a pretty cascade half swept by a sheet of pendant willow-branches. Their delicate shadows, broken with long gleams of sunshine falling aslant the water, told Zulima that the time of Ross's return was fast drawing near. Now she became cruelly restless. Like some bright spirit sent down to trouble the waters at her feet, she wandered along the broken bank, gathered quantities of wild-flowers but to cast them away at the least noise, and frightening the ground-birds from their nests with reckless inattention to their cries, always listening, and half the time holding her breath with impatient longing for something to break the entire solitude that encompassed her.

It came at last—the distant tread of a horse, more than one, Zulima's quick ear detected that in an instant. Still she could not be mistaken in the hoof-tread; she had heard it a hundred times when her heart was beating tumultuously as then, but without the sharp anxiety that now sent the blood from her cheek and lips while she listened. Ross had ridden her husband's horse to the city that day, and she would have been sure of his approach though a troop of calvary had blended its tramp with the well-known tread.

Zulima started from her motionless attitude and, springing up the bank, stood sheltered by the willow-branches, waiting for Ross to pass the bridge, when she would demand her letter. There she stood, trembling with keen impatience, eager and yet afraid of the sharp disappointment that might follow.

How leisurely those two horsemen rose toward the bridge! They were conversing earnestly, and the animals they rode moved close together, as if the riders were intent on some subject to which they feared giving full voice even in that profound solitude. They crossed the bridge at a walk, and without seeming quite conscious how it happened, the two men checked their horses close by the willows, and continued their conversation.

With one foot strained back and the other just lifted from the turf, ready to spring forward, Zulima had watched them coming, but somehow her heart sunk as they drew near, and without knowing it, she allowed that eager foot to sink heavily on the turf again, and shrinking timidly within her shelter, she waited with a beating heart for the conversation to be checked, that she might come forward without intrusion.

"Zulima!" they had used that name once, twice, before her agitation permitted the fact to convey any impression to her mind. But with the name was coupled another that would almost have aroused her heart from the apathy of death itself.

"We must convey it to her gradually; she must be subdued by degrees," said Ross, smoothing the mane of his horse with one hand.

"Yes," replied the other—the same man who had accompanied Ross on his visit to De Grainges cell—"with her inexperience and impetuous temper, there is no judging what extravagance she might enact. She might even start off in search of him, and then—"

Here a sensation of faintness came over Zulima, and she lost a few words. When the mist cleared from her brain, Ross was speaking.

"He would not see her. You do not know the man—see!"

Ross took a letter from his pocket, and the two held it between them, while Ross once or twice pointed out a paragraph with his finger and commented on it in a voice so low that Zulima could only gather what he said from the expression on his face.

The first words that she could distinguish were: "This silence has already driven her wild; you will have a fine time of it when she hears this gossip about a rival."

"It may not reach her; indeed, how can it?"

"These things always reach head-quarters sooner or later," was the reply, so far as it reached Zulima, for that moment the horse which Ross rode became tired of inaction and shied around suddenly. His rider with difficulty secured the letter, which was crushed in his hand, as he hastened to draw the curb, while an envelope, which had contained it, fluttered to the ground.

"Let it go, let it go. I have all that is important," cried Ross, checking his companion, who was about to dismount, and reining in his impatient steed with difficulty.

The next instant they were both out of sight.

Scarcely had they gone when Zulima sprang from her covert and seized the envelope. It was her husband's writing, addressed to Ross, the post-mark Philadelphia—a letter from her husband and not to her! Zulima held her breath; she looked wildly around, as if in search of something that could explain this mystery; then her eyes fell to the writing again. Tears that seemed half fire, flashed down upon the paper; her lips began to quiver, she covered the fragment of paper with passionate kisses, and then cast it from her, exclaiming wildly, "Not to me—not to me!"

Zulima returned home that day as she had never done before. The slow, creeping pace, so eloquent of depression and baffled hope, that had previously marked her return home, was exchanged for a hurried tread and excited demeanor. She was fully aroused to a sense of wrong, to a knowledge that some mystery existed which involved her own future. All her suspicions were vague and wildly combined with such facts as lay before her, but nonetheless powerful and engrossing.

She found Ross in the hall, standing by the back-door, which opened to the garden and talking to his traveling companion. The conference was checked as she came up, and she heard Ross say, quickly, "Hush! hush! she is here!" Then the two stepped out and sauntered slowly along the garden walk. Zulima followed their footsteps, with the wild fire of excitement burning in her cheeks and eyes.

Ross turned to meet her. His look was calm, his voice compassionate.

"We have heard nothing. There was no letter," he said, interpreting the question that hung on her lips.

"No letter to anyone?"

Ross looked at her keenly. It was a strange question, and startled him. Could the young creature suspect that he was in correspondence with her husband? She might conjecture, but could not know. With this thought he answered her.

"He seems to have forgotten all his friends, for even upon business Mr. Clark communicates with no one."

Zulima parted her lips to answer, but checking herself, she turned away and went to her room. Her previous distrust of Ross was fully confirmed by the false answer that he had given; henceforth she resolved to act for herself.

There was a storm that night; the orange-trees and the thick lime-groves were swept by a hurricane that rocked the old mansion house like a cradle. The rain came down in torrents, dashing against the windows, and sweeping out with the wind in waves of dusky silver. All night long the lightning and the winds wrangled and caroused around the house, kindling up the chamber of Zulima every other moment with a torrent of white flame. She was writing—always writing, or with impatient hands tearing up that which she had done, dissatisfied that language could not be made more eloquent. She lifted her pale face as the lightning came in, sweeping over her loosened hair and her long, white robe, and she longed to dip her pen in the flame, that it might burn the feelings that were heaving her bosom upon the paper, and kindle like feelings in the soul of her husband. Sometimes the lightning found tears upon her cheek, trickling down from her long eyelashes and raining over her paper in torrents that would have quenched the fiery words she so longed to write; sometimes it found a smile parting her lips, and a gleam of ineffable affection glowing in her eyes. Changeful as the storm was that beautiful face, where the tumult of her feelings was written plainly as the tempest could be traced upon the sky.

At last Zulima became wholly absorbed in that which she was writing. Her pen flew across the paper; her eyes grew luminous with ardent light. She no longer startled at some new outbreak of the storm; when the lightning flashed over her, she only wrote the faster, as if inspired by the flame. A great magnolia-tree near the window, with all its garniture of leaves, its massive branches and broad, white blossoms, was uprooted and hurled down upon the house, shaking it furiously in every timber. That instant Zulima was placing her name to the letter, which in all this whirl of the elements she had written to her husband. She dropped the pen with a scream, and darted toward the window. The sash was broken and choked up by a great branch of the magnolia, through whose dark leaves and white blossoms, crushed and broken together, the lightning shot like a storm of lurid arrows. The broken glass, the rent foliage, white and green, fell around Zulima as she thrust aside the massive bough with both hands, and looked forth. It was completely uptorn, that fine old tree! The fresh earth, matted to its roots, rose high in the air, dripping with rain, and its great trunk crushed the wicker garden-seat into atoms where she and her husband had sat together the evening before his departure. Heart-sick and faint, Zulima drew back. The letter to her husband lay upon the table, and near it the taper flared, throwing a jet of flame over the delicate writing.

Pale and trembling, for the fall of that old magnolia had terrified her like a prophecy, Zulima folded the paper and directed it. But how her hand shook; the name of her husband was blurred as she wrote it, and with a deep sigh she took up the sealing-wax and held it in the half-extinguished light. Her hand was very unsteady, and a drop or two of the hot wax fell upon her palm and wrist, burning into the delicate flesh like a blood-spot. Still, in her sad preoccupation, Zulima felt nothing of the pain but sealed her letter just as her light flared out, and sat down in the gloom to wait for morning.

Two weary hours she spent in that dark stillness, for the hurricane having done its work, passed off as suddenly as it had arisen, leaving the night hushed and still, like a giant lying down to rest after a hard fight.

When the morning came, with its sweet breath and rosy light, Zulima arose. Hastily binding up her hair, and changing her dress, she took up her letter and left the house. All around the old mansion was littered with vestiges of the storm. She was obliged to make her way through branches heavy with drenched blossoms and young fruit—fragments of lusty vines that had cast their grateful shade around the dwelling but a day before. Oak boughs wrenched away from the neighboring groves and masses of torn foliage lay heaped upon the doorstep and along the walk; these she was compelled to traverse on her passage to the highway.

Scarcely heeding the ruin around her, Zulima walked on toward the city; her delicate slippers were speedily saturated with wet, and at another time that tenderly nurtured frame must have yielded to the discomfort and fatigue of her unusual exertion. But she had an object to attain—an object which depended wholly upon herself; and when a woman's heart and soul is in an effort, when was her strength known to give way? The old cathedral clock was striking six when Zulima entered New Orleans; a few negroes were abroad, going to or from the markets, and around the wharves arose a confused sound as of a hive of bees preparing to swarm. At another time Zulima might have been startled at finding herself the only white female abroad in a great city, but now she only drew the folds of black lace more closely over her bonnet and walked on. With her own hands she mailed the letter which conveyed, as it were, her soul to the husband who seemed to have forgotten her. A sigh broke up from her heart as the folded paper slid from her hand into the yawning mail-bag, and then, with a feeling of relief born of her own exertions, she turned away.

"I have trusted no one; he will get my letter now," she murmured over and over again during her rapid walk home, and with that vivid reaction so common to imaginative natures, she became almost happy in the sweet hopes that this reflection aroused to life again. Oh, it is so difficult for the young to feel absolute despair or absolute resignation; both are the fruit of good or evil old age.

Unmolested, as she had left it, Zulima stole back to her chamber. Weary, and yet with a heart more free than it had been for weeks, she flung off her damp garments, and lying down, slept sweetly for an hour. Zulima dreamed that she was sitting with her husband beneath the great magnolia-tree; her babe lay upon the turf laughing gleefully, and, with its little hands in the air, grasping after the summer insects as they flashed overhead. All at once a whirlwind rushed out, as it were, from the depths of the sky, overwhelming her with its violence. She strove to reach her child, but fell upon her face to the earth, shrieking wildly to her husband to save her and it. Then fell upon her one of those dark, fantastic clouds that make our dreams so fragmentary. She felt the magnolia upheave under her and scatter down the fresh earth from its roots till she was half buried. Husband and child both were gone, leaving her prostrate and almost dead, to battle her way through the storm alone—alone! Zulima awoke with these words upon her lips.

It was but a dream. Louisa had entered the chamber and was examining the wet garments that her mistress had flung off, muttering suspiciously to herself as she saw the soiled slippers and other evidences of an early walk.

"What am de meaning ob all dis? What can de missus be about?" she muttered, casting down the raiment that had excited her distrust. The candle almost burned out, the drops of wax on the table, and torn fragments of paper on the floor were new objects of comment. The torn paper was all written upon, and had been gathered up in a grasp and wrenched asunder. The pieces were large, and might be easily combined. The negress could not read, but, with the quick cunning of her race, she saw that something unusual had happened, with which these fragments were connected, so gathering the papers in her apron, she bore them to her master whose spy she was.

It was the noise that Louisa made going out which aroused Zulima from her wretched vision. The young creature started up, thanking God that it was but a dream. In moving about the room, she approached a window opening upon the garden just in time to see Ross follow her woman, Louisa, into the little slave-dwelling which we described in our last chapter.

Zulima lingered by the window. It was half an hour before Ross came forth again; he was followed by the slave woman, and stood conversing with her some time in one of the retired walks. Soon after, the young man who had been Ross's companion from the city the previous day came up, and Louisa seemed to be dismissed. Still the two men conversed earnestly together and, after a time, slowly retired into the slave-dwelling.

Since the previous day Zulima had grown suspicious, and she remarked all these movements with keen interest. Well she might, for that day and hour, in the low slave-dwelling, was written a letter destined to cast black trouble upon her whole life. There, two fiends, fashioned like men, sat down and concocted a foul slander against that innocent young woman which was to cling around her for years and which her full strength might struggle against in vain. The very mail which carried out Zulima's passionate and tender epistle to her husband bore also a wicked slander framed by these two base men. The pleading words, the endearing expressions, that she had folded up fresh from her innermost soul, that he might know how truly she loved him, went jostling, side by side with the fiendish assertion that she, Zulima Clark, had been unfaithful to his love.

And these two letters reached the husband in one package lying close to each other. *He read the slander first.*

Zulima waited, but no answer ever came to her letter. Week after week she lived upon that painful hope which hangs upon the morrow, and still hope mocked her. Then she grew desperate. One day, when Ross came back from the city empty-handed as usual, Zulima had left his house with the avowed intention of seeking her husband in the North.

"Let her go," said the fiend, cooly folding the letter she had left behind. "The mail travels faster than she can; my pretty bird shall find all things prepared for her coming."

Again Ross sat down and wrote to the husband of Zulima, telling him that she fled from his house at night to escape the vigilant watch which had been placed upon her actions. The letter reached its destination and performed its evil work.

———————

Zulima had taken passage for the North, but the brig must lie at its wharf a few hours, and the unhappy young creature was far too restless for confinement in the close cabin. A yearning desire possessed her to go and search for her infant. Though enjoined to caution and strict secrecy, the place of her child's residence had been intrusted to her, and she had found means to see it unsuspected, from time to time, before her husband's departure. Now, when she was going in agony of spirit to seek the father, she could not depart without embracing his child once more, and, with its little hands around her neck, praying God to bless her mission. Urged by these keen desires, Zulima threw a scarf around her, and drawing down her vail, entered the streets of New Orleans. The house where her child lived was in the suburbs, and she was obliged to cross the city. With a quick step she threaded the streets, heedless of observation and only desirous of reaching her child before the brig was ready to sail.

Was it fate, or was it that sublime intuition that belongs to the higher order of feelings, which led poor Zulima by one of those large

Catholic burial-places in New Orleans which seem to open the way to eternity through a paradise of flowers. It must have been the spiritual essence in her nature, for as the young mother passed this beautiful place of death, she looked eagerly through the gates, and something impelled her to enter. A wilderness of tombs, draped and garmented with vines all in blossom, and shrubs that exhaled perfume from every leaf, lay before her, and at that moment death looked so pleasant to poor Zulima that she longed to lie down and let her heart stop beating where so many had found quiet rest. These reflections brought tears to her eyes; she felt them dropping fast beneath her vail, and entered the inclosure that no one might witness her grief. Slowly and sadly she wandered on, forgetful of her purpose and possessed of a vague idea that her errand led no farther. A strange and dreamy sensation crept over her, the vigor of her limbs gave way, and sweeping the purple clusters of a passion flower from one of the marble slabs, she sat down. Zulima put aside her vail, and began to read the inscription upon the tomb while listlessly passing her finger through the deeply-cut letters.

It was an infant's tomb. A child eighteen months old lay beneath the marble. Eighteen months—that was the age of her child, little Myra. She started up. It seemed as if her weight upon the marble could injure the little sleeper. Carefully drawing the passion-vine over the stone again, she turned away and was about to depart. But that instant there came bounding along the vista of a neighboring walk a young child, evidently rejoicing over its escape from some person who might have controlled its actions. In and out through the flowery labyrinth it darted, its chestnut curls floating on the wind, and its blue sash, loose at one end, sweeping the tombs at every turn. The child, at last, felt evidently quite secure from pursuit, for, leaning forward upon one tiny foot, she peered roguishly through the branches and burst into a clear, ringing laugh that sounded amid the stillness like the sudden gush of a fountain.

Through and through Zulima's heart rang that silvery shout; eye, lip, and cheek lighted up to the sound. She reached forth her arms— "Myra! Myra!"

The child heard her name and turned like a startled fawn, still laughing, but afraid that the black nurse had found her. When she saw only a beautiful woman with eyes brimful of tears and outstretched hands, the laugh fled from her lips, and fixing her large brown eyes wonderingly on the strange face for a moment, she drew timidly toward the tomb by which Zulima stood.

"My child! my own dear child!" broke from the lips of that young mother, and sinking upon her knees, she snatched the little girl to her bosom, covering her lips and forehead with kisses.

"Do you love me? Myra, do you love me?" she cried, holding back the face of the infant between both her trembling hands, and gazing fondly on it through her tears. "Do you love me, Myra?"

At first the little girl was startled by the passionate tenderness of her mother, and she struggled to get away from the bosom that heaved so tumultuously against her form. But, as this touching cry for affection broke from Zulima's lips, the child ceased to struggle, and lifting her clear eyes with a look of wondering pity, she clasped her little hands over her mother's neck, and to her trembling lips pressed that little rosy mouth.

"Don't cry so, I do love you!" lisped the child, it its sweet imperfect language.

These pretty words unlocked a flood of tender grief in the mother's heart. She arose with the child in her arms and then sat down upon the tomb. Smiles now broke through her tears, and during fifteen minutes it seemed to Zulima as if she had passed through that place of tombs into paradise, so sweet was the love that flooded her heart with every lisping tone of her child. But for the poor mother there was no lasting happiness. While her bosom was full of these sweet maternal feelings, there came tearing through the shrubbery a negro woman, panting with haste, and shouting in a coarse voice the name of little Myra.

"We must part, my child!" murmured Zulima, turning pale as the woman caught sight of her charge from a tomb which she had

33

mounted to command a view of the grounds, and with a degree of self-command that was wonderful even to herself, she arose and led the little girl forward.

"Oh, Miss Myra, Miss Myra!" cried the negress, snatching up the little girl and kissing her with a degree of eagerness that made poor Zulima shudder. "What should I have done if you had been lost in earnest?"

Myra struggled to get away, and held out her arms to Zulima. How pale the poor mother was! Her eyes sparkled though at this proof of fondness in the child, and taking her from the woman, she kissed her forehead, and leading her a little way off, bent down with a hand upon those bright ringlets, and called down a blessing from God upon her daughter. Ah! these blessings, what holy things they are! The sunshine they pour forth, how certain it is to flow back to the source and fill it with brightness! If "curses are like chickens that always come home to roost," are not blessings like the ringdoves that coo most tenderly in the nest that shelters their birth? For many a day, while tossed upon the waters, Zulima was the happier for having seen and blessed her child.

CHAPTER THREE

THE VILE LETTER

Oh, she was like a fawn, chased to the plain,
Half blind with grief and mad with sudden pain
That plunges wildly in its first despair,
To any copse that offers shelter there.

It was near midsummer when one of the city postmen of Philadelphia entered a large warehouse in the business part of that city. He approached the principal desk with a bundle of papers and letters on one arm, from which he drew a single letter bearing the New Orleans post-mark. A young man who stood at the desk writing what appeared to be business notes, of which a pile, damp with ink, lay at his elbow, took the letter, and thrusting his pen back of one ear, prepared to open it. There was an appearance of great and even slovenly haste about this letter. The paper was folded unevenly. The wax had been dropped upon it in a rude mass, and was roughly stamped with a blurred impression which it would have been difficult to make out. The address was blotted, and everything about it bore marks of rough haste. The young merchant broke open the seal with some trepidation, for the singular appearance of the letter surprised him not a little. He read half a dozen of the first lines, then looking over his shoulder as if afraid some one might see that which he had read, he turned his back to the desk and was soon wholly absorbed in the contents of the epistle. As he turned over the page, you would have seen the color gradually deepen upon his cheeks and even flush up to the forehead, as if there was something in the epistle which did not altogether please him. After a little he folded the letter, compressing his lips the while, and fell into deep thought. The service which this letter required of him was one against which every honest feeling of his heart revolted; but his worldly prospects, his hopes of advancement in life, all depended upon the writer. Ross had been his friend—had placed him in the Philadelphia branch of a great commercial house—and to thwart one of his wishes might prove absolute ruin.

Ross had omitted in that epistle nothing that could persuade or reason into wrong. It was doubtful, he said, even if Clark ever had been married to Zulima; or, being so, if he would not deem it a good service in his friends to relieve him of the obligations imposed by that union. Bitter and cruel were the accusations urged against that poor young wife; and with his interests all with her enemies, joined to a lively desire to think ill of her, in order to justify his conduct to his own heart, this weak and cruel man yielded himself to become the tool of a deeper and far more unprincipled villain than himself. Again and again he perused that letter and at length put it carefully away in his breast-pocket, close to a heart which its evil folds were doomed to harden against the secret whisperings of a conscience that would not be entirely hushed.

Perhaps, had James Smith been given time for after reflection, he might have become shocked with the part that he was called upon to perform; but the letter which opened this wicked scheme to him had been delayed and carried in a wrong direction by the mail, and nearly two weeks had been thus lost after the time when it should have reached him.

Smith had scarcely turned from his desk with the evil letter in his bosom, when another man entered the warehouse and placed a little rose-tinted note in his hand. A vague idea that this note had some connection with the slovenly epistle that he had just read took possession of him, before he broke the drop of pale-green wax that sealed it.

The conjecture proved real—Zulima had written that note. She was in Philadelphia, and hoped through her husband's *protégé* to hear some news of him. Smith had no time for reflection; he was called upon to act at once. He went to the hotel where Zulima was staying. Smith entered the hotel hurriedly, as one who has a painful task to accomplish and wishes it over. He was not villain enough to act with deliberation, or with that crafty coldness which fitted Ross so singularly for a domestic conspirator. When he found himself in the presence of this helpless young mother; when he gazed upon her beauty—dimmed, it is true, by all that she had suffered, but obtaining thereby a soft melancholy that was far more touching than the glow of youth in its full joy can ever be—his heart smote him for the wrong it had meditated against her. He sat down by her side, trembling and almost as anxious as she was.

"My husband," said Zulima, turning her eloquent eyes upon his downcast face, "you know him, sir—he is your friend; tell me where he is to be found."

"Your husband, madam! of whom do you speak?"

"Of Mr. Clark—Daniel Clark—your benefactor and my husband," said Zulima.

"Daniel Clark, lady?"

"I wish to see him—I *must* see him—tell me where he is to be found." Zulima was breathless with impatience; her large eyes brightened, her cheeks took a faint color. She was determined that nothing should keep her from the presence of her husband.

"And you—you are the young lady that went South with him the last time he was here?" said Smith, bending his eyes to the floor and faltering in his speech.

"Yes, I went with him—I was his wife!"

Smith shook his head; a faint smile crept over his mouth. He seemed to doubt her assertion.

Zulima saw it, and her face kindled with indignant passion. "I *am* his wife!" she said.

"The marriage—was it not secret? was it not almost without witness?"

"Secret? yes; but not entirely without witnesses. I can prove my marriage."

"You can prove that some ceremony took place, but can you prove that it was a real marriage ceremony? Indeed, have you never had reason to doubt that it was such?"

"Never, sir," replied Zulima, turning pale. "Never!"

"You were very young, very confiding," replied Smith. "Yet you had some experience in the perfidy of man: this should have made you cautious."

"Oh, my experience! it had been bitter—terrible!" murmured Zulima, clasping her hands, and gazing on the face of her visitor with a look of wild excitement.

"And yet you trusted again!"

Zulima stood up, her face grew white as death. "Do you mean to say, sir, that my husband—that Daniel Clark deceived me like the other?"

"I mean to say nothing," replied Smith, "nothing, save that from my heart I pity you, sweet lady. So much beauty, so trusting; who could help pitying you?"

"You pity me? Oh, father of mercies!" cried the excited young creature, bending like a reed and raising her locked hands to her eyes. "If this thing should be true!" She fell upon a chair; her slight figure waved to and fro in the agony of her doubts.

"Has he written—did he send for you?" questioned Smith, steeling himself against her grief.

"No, no!"

"Is he aware of your coming?"

"No; I shall surprise him. I wished to surprise him!" cried the wretched young creature, dropping her hands.

"I am afraid you *will* surprise him, and unpleasantly, too!" said Smith.

Zulima turned her dry eyes upon him; her lips parted, but she had no power to utter the questions that arose in her heart. A thousand black doubts possessed her. "Why—why?" It was all she could say.

Smith hesitated; he was reluctant to consummate the last act of villainy required of him. It seemed like striking down a lamb, while its soft, trusting eyes were fixed upon his. But he had gone too far, he could not recede now.

"It is rumored—" he said, "it is rumored that Mr. Clark is soon to be married!"

A sort of spasmodic smile parted Zulima's pale lips, till her white teeth shone through. She did not attempt to speak, but sat perfectly still gazing upon her visitor.

"Had your marriage been real, Mr. Clark would not thus openly commit himself."

"Where *is* Mr. Clark?" said Zulima, sharply, and starting as if from a dream.

"He is in Baltimore now."

"And—and the lady?"

"She, too, is in Baltimore."

"And I—I will go there also!"

"You! and after that which you know?"

"If these things are true, I will have them from the lips of my—of Daniel Clark. If they are not true—Oh, father of heaven! then will his wife lie down and die at his feet, die of sorrow that she has ever doubted him."

Smith was startled; he had not anticipated this resolute strength in a creature so young and child-like. Did she see Daniel Clark, he knew that all was lost to those whose interest it was to keep the husband and wife asunder. He attempted to dissuade Zulima from her plan, but this he saw only excited her suspicion without in the slightest degree changing her. All the answer that she made to his arguments was, "I will see my husband; I must have proof of these things!"

Smith would have urged his objections further, but they were interrupted. The room in which they sat was a parlor to which others might claim admission. Just then the door opened, and a young gentleman entered with the easy and confidential air of an old acquaintance. He cast a glance at Zulima, seemed surprised by the terrible agitation so visible in her face, and then fixed his penetrating eyes searchingly upon Smith.

"You do not seem well," he said, approaching Zulima, and Smith could detect that in his voice which ought to have startled Zulima long before. "Has anything gone amiss?" and he cast a stern look on Smith.

"I am not well!" said Zuliman, and tears came into her eyes.

"But you seem worse than ill—you look troubled."

"Zulima lifted her eyes up with a painful smile, but made no answer.

The young man looked distressed; he stood a moment before Zulima, and then walking toward a window, began to drum on the panes with his fingers, now and then casting furtive glances toward the sofa where Zulima and Smith were sitting.

Smith arose to go. A new gleam of light had broken upon him—he saw and understood more than that fated young creature had even guessed at.

"Then you are determined to undertake this journey?" he said, in a low voice.

"Yes!"

"When will you set out?"

"To-morrow!"

"Alone?"

Zulima unconsciously glanced toward the young man; he had been very kind to her, and it seemed hard to start off utterly alone.

"I don't know," she faltered. "Yes, I shall take the journey alone."

"Your health seems delicate, you are so young," urged Smith, reading her thoughts and hoping that she would be guided by the first imprudent impulse.

"I am young, I am not well—but I shall go alone," she answered, with gentle firmness.

The young man at the window seemed restless. He walked toward a table, and taking up two or three books, cast them back again with an air of impatience. Smith observed this and smiled quietly within himself as he went out. Zulima saw nothing: she only knew that she was very, very wretched. Casting her arms over the back of the sofa, she buried her face upon them and groaned in bitter anguish.

Zulima was so lost in the agony of her feelings that she did not know when the young man placed himself by her side. She was quite unconscious of his approach till her hand was in his, and his voice uttered her name in tones that made her nerves thrill from head to foot. Tenderness had given to that voice an intonation startlingly like the low tones of Daniel Clark when love most softened his proud nature.

She started and looked wildly at the young man, her hand trembling in his—her lips parted in a half smile—the delusion had not quite left her.

"Zulima, what is it that troubles you? Oh, if you only knew, if you could but guess, how—how it wrings my heart to see you thus! What has the man been saying to wound you?"

"To wound me?" repeated Zuliman, recovering from the sort of dream into which his voice had cast her, and drawing her hand away. "Oh, everybody says things to wound me, I think!"

"But I never have."

"No, I believe not," replied Zulima, listlessly. "I believe not."

"And never will," urged the young man, regarding her with a look of deep tenderness.

"I don't know," was the faint reply, and Zulima's face fell back on her folded arms again.

The young man arose and began to pace up and down the room; many a change passed over his features meanwhile, and he cast his eye from time to time upon the motionless figure of Zulima with an expression that revealed all the hidden love, the wild devotion with which he regarded her. He sat down again and took her passive hand. She did not attempt to withdraw it. She did not even seem to know that it was in his.

"Do you know how I love you—how, with my whole life and strength, I worship you Zulima?" he said. "There is nothing on earth that I would not do, could it give you a moment's happiness."

Zulima slowly unfolded her arms, and, lifting her head, looked earnestly in his face with her eyes. She did not seem to understand him.

"Oh, you must have seen how I love you," he said passionately.

Zulima smiled—oh, what a mocking smile! how full of wild anguish it was! "Another!" she said, "so now another loves me."

"No human being ever loved as I love you, Zulima," said the young man, in that pure, sweet voice, which had so affected her before.

"That is a marvel," said Zulima, with a bitter smile. "Others have loved me so well. You do not know how others have loved me."

"I do not wish to know any thing except how I can make you happier than you are, Zulima."

"If you wish to make me happy, do not even mention love to me again. The very word makes me faint," said Zulima. "I am ill—I suffer. Do not, I pray you, talk this way to me. I can not bear it."

"I will say nothing that can distress you," replied the young man gently, but with a look of grief.

Zulima reached forth her hand. It was cold and trembling

"Farewell!" she said, very kindly; "I shall go away tomorrow. Farewell!"

He would not release her hand.

"You are not going far—you will return in a few days. Promise me that you are not saying farewell forever."

"I do not know—the Father in heaven only knows what will become of me; but you have been kind to me—very. You have respected my unprotected lot. You did not know how wrong it was to love me. I can not blame you. When I say farewell thus, I much fear that it is to the only true friend that I have in the world. You could not wish me to feel more regret than I do. Is it not casting away all the unselfish kindness—all the real friendship that I have known for a long, long time?"

"But this love—this idolatry, rather?" persisted the young man, "must it be forever hopeless? Shall I never see you again?"

"It is wrong, therefore should be hopeless," replied Zulima. "You do not know what trouble it would bring upon you."

"Why wrong?—why should it bring trouble upon me?"

"Should we ever meet again, you will know. Everybody will know why it is wrong for you to love me. Now I must go."

Zulima drew away her hand, using a little gentle force; and while the young man was striving to fathom the meaning of her words, she opened the door and disappeared.

Every way was poor Zulima beset. The false position in which the concealment of her marriage had placed her, made itself cruelly felt at all times. She had taken a long journey, alone and entirely unprotected. Young and beautiful—to all appearance single—she was naturally exposed to all those attentions that a creature so lovely and unprotected was sure to receive, even against her will. In the young man whom she had just left, those attentions gradually took a degree of tender interest which, but for her state of anxious preoccupation, she must have observed long before, as others less interested had not failed to do. But she had literally given the devotion, so apparent to others, no thought. Knowing herself to be bound by the most solemn ties to the man who seemed to have forgotten her, she never reflected that others knew nothing of this, or that she might become the object of affectionate, nay, passionate regard, such as the man had just declared.

Now it only served to add another pang to the bitterness of her grief; heart-wounded, neglected as she had been, it was not in human nature to be otherwise than flattered and very grateful for devotion which soothed her pride, and which in its possessor was innocent and honorable. But even these feelings gained but a momentary hold upon her; they were followed by regret and that shrinking dread which every new source of excitement is sure to occasion where the heart has been long and deeply agitated. She went away then with a new cause of grief added to those that had so fatally oppressed her.

————————

Zulima reached Baltimore in the night. Weary with travel and faint with anxiety, she took a coach at the stage-house and went in search of the hotel where she learned that her husband was lodged. As she drove up to the hotel a private carriage stood at the entrance; a negro in livery was in the seat, and another stood with the carriage door in his hand, watching for someone to come down the steps. The door opened, and by the light that streamed through, Zulima saw her husband richly dressed as if for some assembly. One white glove was held loose in his hand with an embroidered opera-cap, which he put upon his head as he came quickly down the steps.

Zulima was breathless; she leaned from the window of her hackney-coach, and would have called in him aloud, but her tongue clove to her mouth. She could only gaze wildly on him, as just touching the step of his carriage with one foot he sprung lightly in. the door closed with a noise that went through Zulima's heart like an arrow. She saw the negro spring up behind the carriage; the lamps flashed by her eyes, and while everything reeled before her, the coachman of her own humble hack had opened the door.

"No, no, I do not wish to get out," she said, pointing toward the receding lamps with her finger. "Mount again and follow that carriage."

The man hastily closed the door, and, mounting his seat, drove rapidly after Mr. Clark's carriage. Zulima was now wild with excitement; the blood seemed to leap through her heart, her cheeks burned like fire. She gasped for breath when a turn in the streets took those carriage-lamps an instant from her sight.

They came in sight of a fine old mansion-house, standing back from the street and surrounded by tall trees; an aristocratic and noble dwelling it was, with the lights gleaming through its windows, and those rare old trees curtaining its walls with their black branches, now gilded and glowing with the golden flashes of light that came through all the windows. The house was evidently illuminated for a party—one of those pleasant summer-parties that are half given in the open air. A few lamps hung like stars along the thick branches that curtained the house and glowed here and there through a honeysuckle arbor, or in a clump of bushes, just lightly enough to reveal the dewy green of the foliage, without breaking up the quiet evening shadows that lay around them. Mr. Clark's carriage stopped before this noble mansion, and Zulima saw him pass lightly into the deep old-fashioned portico while her vehicle was yet half a block off.

"Do you wish to get out here?" said the coachman, going again to the door. "The carriage that you ordered me to follow does not seem to be going any farther."

"I know, I see," said Zulima. "Not now, I will wait. Draw off to the opposite side of the street, and then we shall be in nobody's way."

The man expressed no surprise at her strange orders, but drove back to the shadowy side of the street and waited, standing by the door a moment, to learn if she had any further directions to give. Zulima bent from the window; she was terribly agitated and her voice trembled.

"Whose house is this?" she said, hurriedly.

The man told the owner's name. It was one celebrated in the history of our country; and Zulima remembered with a pang that the daughters of that house were among the most lovely and beautiful women of America. Smith had told her that her husband was about to be married. Was it in that stately old mansion house that she must search for a rival? How her cheek burned, how her lip trembled, as she asked herself the question!

"Did you know," she said, addressing the man, "did you know the gentleman who just went in yonder?"

"Oh yes, everybody here knows Mr. Clark," said the man. "I guessed well enough where his carriage was driving to, when it started from the hotel. He is going to marry one of the young ladies; at least the papers say so."

Zulima drew back into the carriage; it seemed as if she would never breathe again. She sat like a famished bird, gazing on the house without the wish or power to move.

There seemed to be a large party assembled; gayly dressed people were constantly gliding before the window, and she could see the gleam of rich wines and trays of fruit, as they were borne to and fro by the attendants. Sometimes a couple would saunter out into the deep old portico, where she could see more distinctly by the wreath of colored lamps, festooned with trumpet-flowers, roses, and honey-suckles that fell like a curtain overhead. Zulima saw one couple after another glide into the flowery recess, and away again, as if the music that came pouring through doors and windows were too exciting for a prolonged *tete-a-tete*. Still she kept her eyes fixed upon the spot; she was certain that Mr. Clark would be among those who haunted that flower nook, so like a cloud of butterflies. She knew his tastes well. Sure enough, while her eyes were fixed on the open doors, through which the background of the portico was flooded with golden light, she saw Mr. Clark come slowly down the hall, not alone—oh, how she had hoped for that—but with a beautiful woman leaning on his arm, leaning heavily with that air of languid dependence which so often marks the first development of passion. His head was bent, and he seemed to be addressing her in a low voice; and though he smiled while speaking, Zulima could see that in repose his face was grave, almost sad. It only lighted up when those large blue eyes were lifted toward him. They sat down in the portico, and seemed to converse earnestly—ten minutes, half an hour, and hours—thus long did the two sit side by side under that canopy of lighted blossoms, and then Zulima could watch them no longer. A heavy faintness crept over her, and in a dull, low voice she asked the coachman to drive her back to the hotel.

Poor Zulima! she hoped to see her husband alone in that portico, if it was only for one minute. How long, how patiently had she waited, and that beautiful woman never left his side for a moment. It was very cruel.

When Zulima left her room early the next morning, she found Mr. Smith, who seemed to have just left the stage-coach. She knew him at once, and he recognized her with great cordiality.

"I have come—," he said, in a low, friendly voice, "I have come in hopes of seeing you with Mr. Clark. He is in the hotel, I hear."

"He is," said Zulima. "I saw him last night!"

Mr. Smith turned pale, but there was a deep depression in Zulima's voice and manner that re-assured him the interview could not have been a happy one, to leave that cheek so hueless, the eyes so heavy—he was not yet too late.

"I saw him," said Zulima, "but he did not know it. Today, within another hour, I shall know why he has treated me thus; tell me how I can get a message conveyed to him."

"I will convey it; I will urge your cause."

"Only tell him I am here; I want no one to plead for me with *him*. Only do that, and I will thank you much."

"I will do that, and more," said Smith, bowing.

What influence was it that kept Mr. Clark so wakeful on the night when Zulima, his young wife, slept beneath the same roof with

47

himself? He knew nothing of her presence—he felt not the bitter tears that almost blistered her pale cheek as she tried to stop thinking of him, the sobs that shook her frame till the bed trembled under it— none of them reached his ear. It was not any remembrance of the lovely young being who had hung upon his arm and sat beside him in that flower-lit portico but a short time before: her beauty had pleased him, her conversation had wiled away a little of that time which was often spent in bitter thoughts, since he had begun to receive the letters of Ross and to yield credence to the reports regularly sent him of the estrangement and faithlessness of his young wife.

She had fled now—fled from his friend's roof, and come northward no doubt to obtain greater freedom, and escape the vigilance of those he had placed about her. Thus ran the last letter that Clark had received from his friend.

Clark read the letter over, after he returned home that night, for something seemed constantly whispering of Zulima; he could not drive her from his mind. It seemed to him as if some great mistake had arisen, as if he had not read the letters of his friend aright. No, when he perused this letter again, it was clearly written; nothing ambiguous was there, nothing hinted. His wife had ceased to love him; she had fled. Still there was something in his heart that would not be thus appeased; the mysterious presence of this young creature seemed to haunt his room, haunt the innermost chambers of his heart. He thought of the letter she had written him, and which he had burned while under the terrible influence of his friend's epistle. He began to regret now, to wish that he had at least seen the contents of that letter; still his friend was dispassionate, just—why should this calm report be doubted? A report evidently wrung from him by a strong sense of duty.

Mr. Clark slept little that night; his better angel was abroad. Zulima, too, was weeping beneath the same roof; he knew it not, but still he could not sleep!

In the morning Smith came to the chamber where Mr. Clark was sitting at breakfast. His face was sad; he seemed ill at ease.

"I thought it best to come and bring this news to you first; it might save you from great embarrassment."

"What news?—what embarrassment?" said Clark, who had no idea that Smith knew any thing of Zulima, or her connection with him. "Surely nothing has gone wrong in the business?"

"No, but the young lady who says she knew you in New Orleans—that she has claims upon you!"

Mr. Clark turned deathly white; this sudden mention of his wife unnerved him.

"And is she in Philadelphia?—where is she?—how came she to find you out?"

"I do not know; she sent me a note, and I went to her hotel."

"Was she alone—was she alone?" questioned Mr. Clark, starting up.

"No, not quite alone," replied Mr. Smith, with a meaning smile. "I saw only one person with her, a young and remarkably handsome man."

Mr. Clark sunk to his chair as if a bullet had passed through his heart. "Go on," he said, after a moment, "go on, I am listening."

"This lady, sir, seemed determined to see you; she came on here—she is now in Baltimore."

"And her companion?" said Mr. Clark, with a ghastly smile.

"No," replied Smith, "I think she would not do that. She wishes to see you; I do not know what her object is."

"I will not see her; I will never see her again," said Mr. Clark, and his face looked like marble. "If she needs anything, supply her; she is, sir, the mother of my child; she is—but I will not talk of it. Let her want for nothing—she is my wife."

"You will not see her then?"

"No, it is enough." Mr. Clark rang the bell—a man entered. "Have my carriage brought up at once; I shall set out for Washington. Mr. Smith, you know how to act. Save me from a repetition of this: you see how it tortures me. I loved that young creature—I thought, fool, madman, that I was—but she seemed to love me."

Mr. Clark went into another room; he could not endure that other eyes should witness his emotion. The coachman now came up; his proud master understood that everything was ready, and without speaking a word, left his apartments. He stepped into his carriage; he was gone—gone without hearing the wild shriek that broke from the lips of that poor young wife, who had caught one glimpse of him from her window. She shook the sash—she strove to call after him, but her arms trembled, her voice was choked. With all her effort she made but little noise; those in the next room heard nothing of it, till she fell heavily on the floor. Mr. Smith found her there, lying like a corpse rigid and insensible. Then his heart smote him—then would he have given worlds that the falsehoods which brought all this misery had not been uttered. He had tried to think ill of his victim, to believe that between her and her husband there was neither love nor sympathy. How had the last hour undeceived him. Maddened by doubt and jealousy, his benefactor had not even attempted to conceal the anguish occasioned by what he deemed perfidy of his wife; and she—was she not there, cold as marble, white as death, prostrate at his feet?

But he could not go back—his evil work must be full accomplished. Now to shrink or waver, would be to expose himself; that he could not contemplate for a moment. Zulima became sensible, at last. It was a long time, but finally she opened her eyes and sat up. "He is gone," she said lifting her heavy eyes to Smith.."He is gone without a word of explanation."

"What could he explain but that which he would not wish to say face to face with his victim? He has deceived you with a mock marriage. I knew that it would prove so. You are free; you are wealthy, if you choose. Be resigned; there is no redress."

"No redress!" Zulima repeated the word over and over again. "No redress! I thought myself his wife; I am the mother of his child; O God! Myra, Myra, my poor, poor child—" ★ ★ ★ ★ ★ ★ ★

They were parted—Zulima solemnly believed that she had never been the wife of Daniel Clark, that she was free—oh, how cruelly free—and another loved her. Wounded in her pride, broken in spirit, outraged, humiliated, utterly alone; was it strange that the poor torn heart of that young creature at length became grateful for the affection that her grief and her desolation had excited? She told him all, and still that young man loved her, still he besought her to become his wife; and she, unhappy woman—consented.

There was to be no secrecy—no private marriage now; in the full blaze of day robed in satin, glossy and white as the leaves of a magnolia, her magnificent tresses bound with white roses, her bridal vail looped to the curls upon her temple with a snowy blossom, and falling over her, wave after wave, like a cloud of summer mist. Thus went Zulima Clark forth to her last bridal. It was a mournful sight; that young girl so beautiful, so fated, standing before the altar, her large eyes surcharged with sorrowful remembrances of the past, and her poor heart heaving with a wild presentiment of coming evil, till the rose upon her bosom, and the pearls upon her throat, trembled as if a wind were passing over them. It was a mournful, mournful wedding; for there, Zulima, the wife of Daniel Clark, sealed the perfidy of her enemies. Beautiful bride, innocent woman, thine was a hard destiny!

CHAPTER FOUR

VILLAINY EXPOSED

Once again they met,
And then they saw, each in the other's heart,
And the black falsehood that had sever'd them
Rose palpable and hideous to the thought.
Hot tears were shed—sad blessings mutely given!
They met, and parted—he went to meet his death,
And she to weep o'er bitter memories!

Zulima made her home in the South, and there also, after years of wandering, came Daniel Clark—weary with excitement, and unhappy with a sense of bitter loneliness. In the first moments of his anger against Zulima, he had made his will, giving all his vast possessions to an aged relative, and making the false friends who had caused his misery executors of that will. And this was the deep game for which these men had staked their souls—these possessions and the control over them. No matter though the fair wife was crushed to the earth; no matter though that beautiful child, in all her infant unconsciousness, was despoiled of her just inheritance. It was for this they had toiled in darkness; it was for this they had heaped falsehood upon falsehood, wrong upon wrong.

But Clark had returned to New Orleans, not to pass a week and away again, as before, but to control his own business—and in New Orleans was Zulima. They might meet, still it was unlikely, for she was proud and sensitive as ever, and lived in the bosom of a new family and was girded around by new and powerful affections. Looking upon Clark as a heart-traitor, one who had betrayed her unprotected state, and trifled alike with her reputation and her love, she shrank from a thought of the past. The wrong that she believed to have been practiced upon her was so terrible that she shuddered at the retrospection. Without one shadow of hate or hope of revenge to perpetuate the struggle that had been so heart ending at first, the only effort that she made was to obtain forgetfulness.

Zulima knew not that Clark had arrived at New Orleans, but a strange inquietude came over her. Thoughts of the sweet and bitter past made her restless day and night; she was haunted by a constant desire to see her child—the child of Daniel Clark; from this innocent creature, wrong and absence in the father had failed to alienate her love.

A little out from New Orleans was a pretty country-house, surrounded by ornamental grounds and embowered in tropical trees. It was a small dwelling, secluded and beautiful as a bower; works of art, rare books, and light furniture, befitting the climate, gave an air of refinement and grace within; passion-flowers, briery roses, and other clinging vines draped the cottage without. An avenue of orange and lime trees led to the front door, and behind was a small garden, cooled by the rain that fell perpetually from a fountain near the center, and glowing with tea-roses, lilies, and a world of those blossoms that grow most thrifty and fragrant in the warm South.

Among these beautiful grounds little Myra Clark had been at play since the breakfast-hour. She had chased the humming-birds from their swarming places in the arbors and rose-hedges; she had gathered golden-edged violets from the borders, and leaping up with a laugh to the orange-boughs that drooped over the gravel-walk, had torn down the white blossoms and mellow fruit to crowd with the flowery spoil that she had gathered in the skirt of her muslin dress. And now with her lap full of broken flowers, fruit, torn grass, and pebble-stones, the child cast herself on the rich turf that swelled up to the brink of the fountain, and pressing her dimpled hands and warm cheek upon the marble, lay in smiling idleness, watching the goldfish, as they darted up and down the limpid waters, her soft brown eyes sparkling with each new flash of gold or crimson that the restless little creatures imparted to the waters. Now she would cast a broken rose-bud or a tuft of grass into the fountain, and her laugh rang out wild and clear above the bell-like dropping of the water in the marble basin, if she could detect some fish darting up like a golden arrow to meet her pretty decoy. Thus lay the child; thus fell the bright water-drops around; and thus, a little way off, dropped the fruit- and flower-laden boughs, when the sweet tranquility was disturbed by a footstep. Down one of the gravel-walks came a man, bearing upon his noble features an air of proud sadness, his very step denoting habitual depression, as he moved quietly and at a slow pace toward the fountain. It was not a look of ill-health that stamped so forcibly the air and demeanor of this man. His frame was still strongly knit, his step firm as iron, but upon his brow was that deep-settled shadow which a troubled heart casts up to the face, and the locks that shaded it were sprinkled with the premature snow which fails early over a brain tortured with unspoken regrets. Thus sorrowful, but still unbowed in his spirit, appeared Daniel Clark, as he moved quietly toward the fountain where his child was at play.

Myra was busy with her gold-fish, laughing and coquetting with them through the waves. She saw nothing but their golden flash; she heard nothing but the light drops that dimpled and clouded the water around them. Thus for several minutes the proud and saddened man stood gazing upon his daughter.

She saw him at last, and then with a faint cry the little creature cast away the contents of her frock, and sprang up. Half in joy, half in timid surprise, she stood gazing upon his face. The pupils of her eyes dilated till they were almost black, her white arms seemed trembling with restraint, as if the suddenness of his appearance had checked the first quick impulse. She was only waiting for one smile to spring like a bird to his bosom.

"Myra!"

The firm voice of Daniel Clark gave way as he uttered the name of his child. His eyes grew dim with tears, and he reached forth his trembling arms. She sprang with a single bound to his embrace; she wreathed his neck strongly with her arms and pressed upon his lips, his cheeks, and his moist eyes, kisses that, from the lips of a beautiful child, seem like the pouring of dew and sunshine from the cup of a flower.

"Oh, you are come again!" she said, placing her warm hands on each side his face, and looking with the smiling confidence of childhood into his eyes. "They told me that you would not come to see us any more for a long, long time."

"And are you glad to see me, darling?" said Mr. Clark, drawing his hand caressingly down the disheveled brightness of her hair. "You seem glad, my little Myra?"

"Seem—why—I am glad—so very, very glad, my own, own—" the child hesitated.

"Papa—will you not call me papa, this once?" said the agitated father, and upon his pale cheek there came a flush, as he said this to the child.

"Oh, but they tell me that you are my godfather, and that is not a papa, you know," said the child, shaking her head with an air of pretty thoughtfulness.

"Perhaps it is as well," murmured the father, and his look grew sad.

Myra bent down and looked into his eyes, smiling.

"Don't look so sorry," she said, "I will call you papa, if you like. Papa! dear papa! there, now!"

But even the childish caress, accompanied as it was by a voice and look of the most winning sweetness, failed to dispel the sadness that had fallen upon the father's heart. Perhaps the very loveliness of the child did but deepen that sadness, by reminding him of its mother. Let this be as it may, Mr. Clark sat down by the fountain with the little girl in his arms, but he remained silent, thus chilling the little creature whose arms were about his neck, and she too became hushed, as it were, by the gloom into which he fell. During several minutes the father and child remained thus wrapped in silence. At last he spoke in a low and troubled voice, kissing the forehead of the child.

"Myra, do you love me?"

"Indeed, indeed I do," said the little girl, laying her cheek to his. "Better almost than anybody else in the wide world, if you are only my godfather."

"And whom—" here Mr. Clark's voice faltered—"and whom can you love better, Myra?"

"Oh," said the child, shaking her head with a pretty mysterious air, "there is somebody that I love so much, a pretty, beautiful lady, who comes to me so often, and so strangely, just like one of the fairies nurse tells me about. Sometimes she will be a long, long time, and not come at all. Then, while I am playing among the trees, she will be close to me before I think of it. She kisses me just as you do, and once—that, too, was so like—" the child paused, and seemed pondering over something in her mind.

"What was so like, Myra?" said Mr. Clark, in a faint voice, for his heart misgave him.

"Why, I was just thinking," said the child thoughtfully, "this pretty lady wanted me to call her mamma, just as you wanted me to call you papa, you know, only in fun."

"And did you call her that?"

"Yes, but I never will again—no, never in the world; for, do you think, she began to cry like anything the moment I put my arms round her neck and said 'mamma!' You can't think how she did cry, and after asking me, too."

Mr. Clark turned away his head; the child's earnest look troubled him.

"She knew well enough that it was all fun," persisted the child, "and yet she kept on crying all I could do."

"Oh, such words are bitter, bitter fun," muttered Mr. Clark, tortured by the innocent prattle of the child.

"I did not mean any harm; the lady asked me to call her 'mamma,' but I never will again," said Myra, drooping under what seemed to her the displeasure of her best friend.

"Oh yes, Myra, you must love this lady; you must call her any thing she pleases," said Mr. Clark, with a burst of emotion that startled the little girl. "Be good to her; be gentle and loving as if—as if it was not fun when you call her 'mamma.' You will be good to her; promise me, my darling, that you will."

"But she will not ask me again. It is a long, long time since the lady has been here," answered the child thoughtfully. "Perhaps she will not come any more."

"Perhaps," said Mr. Clark, with a voice and look of painful abstraction.

A slight noise in a distant part of the garden drew the child's attention. She started, and bending eagerly forward looked down a winding path sheltered by the orange trees.

"See!" cried the child, pointing down the path with her finger, while her eyes sparkled like diamonds. "Didn't I say that she always came like a fairy? Didn't I tell you so?"

Clark followed the child's finger with his eyes, and there coming up the path rapidly, and with eager haste in her look and manner, he saw Zulima, the wife of his bosom, the mother of his child. For the world, that proud man could not have risen to his feet; his strength utterly forsook him. He attempted to remove Myra's arm from his neck, but even that he failed to accomplish, so profound was his astonishment, so overpowering was his agitation.

A tree stood close by the fountain, overrun and shadowed by the convolutions of a passion-flower vine that fell like a curtain around it, concealing the father and child as Zulima came up. Thus it happened that without any preparation, the wronged wife and the deceived husband stood face to face, breathless and pale as statues in a graveyard. The child clung to her father's neck. Her large eyes dilated, and her face grew crimson with fear. She was frightened by the terrible pallor of Zulima's face.

Mr. Clark arose pale as death, and trembling in every limb, he placed the child gently on the grass, and approaching Zulima held forth his hand.

She took it, but her fingers were like marble, and like marble was the cold smile that went in a spasm of pain across her lips.

"Zulima, will you not speak to me?"

Oh, what a flood of bitter waters did that gentle voice unlock in Zulima's heart. Her limbs began to shake, her hands quivered like aspen leaves, and a look of unutterable distress fell upon her face.

"To what end should I speak?" she said, in a low and husky voice. "I have no wish to reproach you, and what but reproaches can you expect from me?"

A bitter smile disturbed the pallor of Daniel Clark's face, and a bitter intonation was blended with the mournful cadence of his voice.

"Reproaches, Zulima, are for slight wrongs; but slight or deep, I deserve none at your hands. While you—oh, woman, woman, how have you betrayed the deep love, the honor which I gave you in holy trust. Neither will I reproach; but when I look upon your face, still young, full of beauty, and bearing the old look of innocence, it forces me to think of the vows you have broken, the mockery you have cast upon our marriage."

"Our marriage," repeated Zulima. Again her lips were distorted with a smile mournful and bitter, and clasping her hands she wrung them nervously together.

"Why do you smile thus? Why do you repeat thus bitterly the words that I have spoken?" said Clark, regarding her wild agitation with wonder. "When I speak of our marriage, you do not shrink or tremble as one who has profaned a holy rite, but your eye is full of scorn, your lips curl with bitter smiles. Zulima, are you indeed so lost that the mention of ties that bound us once, and that legally bind us yet, ties that you, unhappy woman, have broken and dishonored, can only awake a smile of scorn?"

Zulima stood motionless, her hands clasped, her eyes dilating; the truth was struggling to her heart.

"Speak to me, speak to me again," she cried, extending her locked hands imploringly. "That marriage, you know, you know well, it was all false, all a deception. I never was your wife!"

Mr. Clark drew back—he breathed with difficulty: the truth was breaking upon his soul also—the cruel, terrible truth.

"Speak to me, speak to me," cried Zulima, in a voice of thrilling anguish. "I never was your wife!"

"The God of heaven, at whose altar we were united, can answer that you were my lawfully wedded wife, that you are so now!"

A sharp cry broke from Zulima. She staggered forward a pace, and sat down upon the grass close by her child; covering her face with both hands, she bent it down to her knees, and remained thus motionless and absolutely without breath.

Clark stood gazing upon her, every nerve in his body quivering; the horror that her face had exhibited, that sharp cry, the utter prostration of her energies, all these things were fast unsealing his eyes. He sat down by the unhappy woman and attempted to remove one of the pale hands clasped over her eyes, but she resisted him with a faint shudder, and then through those lashed fringes gushed a flood of tears.

"Zulima, try and compose yourself; make one effort, for, on earth, I feel that this must be our last interview. Shrink not thus! I have never wronged you, or if it prove so not knowingly or willfully."

Zulima shook her head, and sobbed aloud. "There has been wrong, deep, black wrong, somewhere," she said. "I was told that you also had deceived me by a false marriage, that the ceremony we went through was a fraud and I your victim, not a wife."

"And who told you this infamous falsehood?" said Clark, clasping his hands till the blood left them, in the agony of his impatience.

"Ross hinted it; Smith told me so in Philadelphia and in Baltimore. They told me, also, that you were about to marry another; I saw you together with my own eyes. You refused to see me; but for that I had never believed them!"

"And Smith told you this; Ross hinted it," cried Clark, locking his teeth with terrible anger. "These two men whom I have fed, whom—" he paused; the violence of his emotion was too great for words.

But why should we further describe the harrowing scene? It was long before these two unhappy beings could speak with calmness, but at length all was told—the fraud that had kept back their mutual letters, the slow and subtle poison that had been instilled so assiduously into each proud and passionate nature—all. For the first time, Clark learned the sufferings, the passionate love, that had sent his young wife in search of him, her struggles, her despair. Then his own haughty reserve gave way; he laid open his whole heart before her, its history and its anguish. He told her of his wanderings, of the deep and harrowing love; which not even a belief in her faithlessness could wring from his heart. He told her all, and then these proud beings sat again, side by side, looking in each other's faces, and yet separated, oh, how irrevocably!

Then came the time for parting. Zulima must go back to her home, and he—where could he seek shelter from the grief of that terrible moment?

They both arose, and face to face, stood gazing on each other for the last time; neither of them doubted that it was for the last time, on this side the grave. A look of mournful despondency was on their features, their hands were clasped for an instant, and then Zulima turned away, and tottering feebly in her walk, passed from the garden.

He stood watching her till the last flutter of her garments disappeared under the orange-boughs, then he turned away and went forth a broken hearted man. Mother and father both went away, leaving the child alone. Terrified by the scene of anguish passing before her, the little creature had neither moved nor spoken, and in the agony of that last parting she was forgotten. She had no heart for play then. The fish turned up their golden sides in vain, the humming-birds flashed by her quite unheeded; she was gazing after her father, and her eyes were full of tears. All at once, she saw him coming back, walking rapidly; tears were in his eyes also, and, taking her to his bosom, he kissed her forehead, her hair, and her little hands. Myra began to sob piteously. She could feel the swelling of his heart against her form; the hot fever of his lips as they touched her forehead, made her tremble, and cling closer to him. It seemed as if the little creature knew that this was the last time that noble heart would ever beat against hers—as if she felt in her whole being that he was her father. Thus, after a brief struggle, the parent and child parted, and forever.

That night Daniel Clark spent under the roof of his friend, Ross, the very roof that had sheltered his bridal life with Zulima and the birth of her child. He met his false friend calmly, and without any outbreak of the terrible sense of wrong that ached at his heart. He said truly that reproaches are for slight wrongs, only his were too mighty for words. He never once hinted to the traitor that he was aware of his treachery. Perhaps the footsteps of coming death were pressing too heavily upon him, even then, for he whispered to his heart more than once that day, "Vengeance is mine, saith the Lord, and I will repay it."

There was no vengeance in Daniel Clark's thoughts; for death was there already, and he felt that the little time given him on earth would scarcely be sufficient to right the wronged.

In the very chamber where Zulima had sat, amid the storm, writing her last soul-touching letter to her husband, was that husband at midnight, writing as eagerly as she had been. His face was deathly pale one minute, and the next there spread over it a warm red hue, that seemed burning hotly through the flesh. He wrote on, sheet after sheet, linking the pages together as he completed them, with a black ribbon; and, notwithstanding the anguish that shook, and the fever that burned him, the writing, as it flowed from his pen, was firm and even as print.

Toward daylight the document was finished. Two black seals were placed at the last page, then the whole was folded up and carefully sealed. Weary and haggard was Daniel Clark as he arose from his task; the bed stood in a corner of the chamber, cool and inviting, but he approached it not. With a heavy and wavering step, he reached the open window, and folding his arms upon the sill, turned his face to the soft night-air, with a faint groan, and thus he remained till morning.

The next day, Daniel Clark rode into the city and was closeted with several of his old and intimate friends. In the house of one of these friends the others met by appointment, and there Daniel Clark read his last will and testament, making his child, Myra Clark, the heiress to his vast possessions, and there he solemnly declared his marriage with Zulima, that child's mother. After this he sat down in the presence of his friends and chosen executors, and placed his signature to the will that his own hands had written.

When Mr. Clark left them that day, his friends observed that the hand with which he clasped theirs was burning, and that his eyes looked heavy and swollen. They remarked, too, that he had never once smiled during the whole interview; but the occasion was a solemn one, and so they merely gave these things a passing thought, deeming them but the result of some undue excitement.

At nightfall Mr. Clark reached the dwelling of Ross. It had been Zulima's residence, and he yearned to lie down in the room that she had occupied, and to press the same pillow that she had wept upon. All the deep tenderness of his early love for that wronged woman came back to him with a knowledge of her blamelessness. Pride, the great sin of his nature, had been prostrated with the knowledge that he, with all his haughty self-reliance, all his splendor of intellect, had been influenced by base and ungrateful men to wrong the being dearest to him in life. All the manifestation of displeasure that he displayed toward Ross was a desire to avoid his presence, but even that awoke the ever-vigilant suspicion of the man. He had placed menial spies on the steps of Zulima, but in hunting down the sterner game Ross played the spy himself. The plantation which Ross occupied was the property of his patron, and in the dwelling Mr. Clark had always kept his own separate apartments. On returning home that night he entered a little library belonging to these apartments, and opening an escritoire had taken from thence an ebony box, in which were his most valuable papers. After placing the will therein he had carefully locked the escritoire and the room before retiring to his chamber for the night.

At two o'clock the next morning there shone in this library a faint light. By the escritoire stood Ross softly trying a key in the lock, and behind him upon a table rested a dark lantern, so placed that all its rays fell in one direction, leaving most of the room in darkness. Noiselessly the key was turned, and without a sound was the escritoire opened, and the ebony box dragged forth.

The will was the first paper that presented itself on opening the box. Ross took it up, seated himself in Mr. Clark's easy chair, and began to read; nervously glancing over the pages, and starting from time to time if the slightest sound reached his ear.

"As I thought!" he said, in a stern, low voice, dashing his hand against the paper till the sheets rustled loud enough to make him start. "Thus has one day undone the work of years. I knew that something had warped his heart against me!"

Thoughtfully, and with a frowning brow, Ross folded up the will, laid it in its depository, and secured it as before. At first he was tempted to take the light from his lantern and consume it at once, but the rash thought was abandoned after a moment's reflection, for there was danger at any hour that Mr. Clark might detect the fraud and place another will beyond his reach. With his duplicate key and ready access to all the apartments, there was little to dread while the will remained under that roof.

The moment everything was safe, Ross closed his lantern and sat for more than an hour musing in the darkness. When he came forth, there was a deep and gloomy cloud upon his brow; the pale moonbeams fell upon it through the windows, as he passed to his own room, but the moonbeams failed to reveal the black thought that lay hidden beneath that frown. There was more than fraud in that hideous thought.

Mr. Clark slept in Zulima's chamber, upon the couch her delicate limbs had pressed, and upon the pillow where her head had found its sweetest slumbers. Perhaps the fever-spirit grew riotous and strong on the memory which these objects aroused, or it might have been that, without all these reminiscences, the illness that came upon him that night would have proved more painful still. The morning found the heart-stricken man faint and strengthless as a child. A vague dreaminess hung about him, which did not quite amount to delirium, and yet it could not have been said that he was quite conscious of passing events. He talked in a low voice of his wife and child: there was something sad and broken-hearted in every word that he uttered, totally at variance with his usual proud and lofty reserve. He seemed to take little interest in those about him, but murmured gently to himself, and always of them. If this was delirium—and it must have been, so totally was it at variance with his previous manner—there was something exceedingly touching and mournful in it, for the death-bed of that noble and strong man seemed marked by a degree of solemn tenderness that might have befitted the death-pillow of a loving woman.

At first the disease seemed scarcely more than an attack of nervous fever, such as often follows violent excitement. The spirits of heaven who guarded that death-bed alone can tell if neglect or irritation, or deeper and darker causes combined to terminate that slight illness in death. Ross was his attendant; constant and unceasing was the assiduity of his watch. No physician, no friend entered the sick-room, and for three days that noble man lay struggling with death, in the presence of his bitterest enemy, and one faithful old body-servant, who could only watch and weep over the master who was to him almost more than mortal.

Then came the third night, and still the failing man was alone with that one old negro, who would not be sent away; and over him bent the household viper, whose sting had been worse than death. A dim lamp was in the room, and through the open windows came the night air, in soft, sweet gushes, making the muslin drapery tremble in the flaring lamplight.

Daniel Clark turned upon his pillow; his eyes opened wide and he moved his hands in the air, as if seeking to grasp at something. Ross bent over and spoke to him, but the dying man closed his eyes and motioned the traitor away with his hand. The old negro came up, choking back the tears, and bent his gray head gently over his master. Again Clark opened his eyes; a sudden light came into them, and a smile stole over the whole face.

"Bend down," he whispered, "bend close to me, my old servant, for I am dying."

The old man bent his head still lower, holding his breath, and checking the tears that swelled his faithful heart. "Dear master, I listen."

Clark lifted his hand, and grasped that of the old man with a feeble hold.

"My wife—my child! See that no wrong is done them."

The old man looked down upon that ashen face with surprise. "This must be delirium," he thought, "for my poor master had neither wife nor child."

The eyes of the dying man were misty, but he saw the doubt in his servant's face. A look of distress passed over his own, and he made a vain effort to collect the power of speech. But he could only say, "The will—that must tell you—it is below, take it into your own hands the moment I am dead; and take it to—to—"

"To Master Ross?" said the old man, observing that his master's voice was sinking.

"No! no!" These words broke from the dying man with his last breath; he fell back upon the pillow. His hands wandered upward for an instant, and then fell heavily upon the bed. Still his eyes were open—still they were fixed with mournful intensity on the old man's face.

"He is gone!" murmured Ross, bending his ashen face over the ashen face of the dead.

"He is gone!" cried the poor old servant, wringing his hands and sobbing aloud, "he is gone, and without taking the old man with him!" Then the faithful old creature cast himself upon his knees, and taking the pale hand of the dead between his ebony palms, lifted up his voice and wept. While the voice of his grief filled the room, while his faithful heart seemed pouring itself out in tears, Ross turned softly and stole from the room.

A few brief minutes the old negro gave to his sorrow. Then amid his tears he remembered the last words of the dead. He did but pause to close, with reverent hands, the eyes that still seemed regarding him with earnest command. He did but compose the lifeless limbs and draw the sheet over those loved features before he went down to obey the last behest of the dead. The poor old man went forth from the death-chamber, guided by the gray dawn. His tread was slow and mournful. You could scarcely hear him as he passed along, for it seemed to him that the faintest sound might disturb his master.

He reached the library. His hand was upon the latch; he turned it with a cautious regard to sound, not with premeditation, but because the death-scene he had witnessed made the least noise appear to him like sacrilege. But the door remained firm. It was evidently locked within, for through the keyhole streamed a faint light, and with the light came an indistinct sound of rustling papers and the cautious tread of a footstep. The old man bent his eye to the keyhole and looked in. Directly within the range of his vision stood Mr. Clark's escritoire wide open, and by it was Ross searching among the papers in an ebony box, which the old man knew as the repository of his master's most valuable documents. Ross took from this box a voluminous parcel, thrust it in his bosom, and carefully locking the escitoire, held up the light and looked timidly around as if fearful of the very silence. Then, with a quick, noiseless tread, he passed across the room. His face was deathly pale, and the old negro saw that the lamp shook and swaled in his hand. There was a fireplace in the room, but the door commanded no view of it, and the old man strained his sight in vain to secure further knowledge of what was passing within the library. But if his eye was baffled his ear remained, keen, and that was directly startled by the sharp rustle of paper apparently torn apart in haste, then the whole room was framed with a glare of light. There was a sudden and faint crackle as of some hastily kindled flame passing up the chimney. Then all was dark and hushed once more. The lamp seemed extinguished; a little smoke, a faint smell of burnt paper, and that was all the poor old negro ever saw of his master's will.

The old man went back to the chamber, knowing too well that his mission was at an end. He knelt down by that death-couch trembling like a culprit, and heart-sick from a consciousness of his own impotence. "Oh, master, master! forgive me—forgive me!" cried the gray-headed old servant, bending his wrinkled forehead to the hands he had clasped upon the death-couch. "Forgive me that I stayed to cry when I should have obeyed the last order you can ever give the old man. I have seen, I have heard—but who will believe me, master? Am I not a slave?"

"A slave? yes; go hence, and forever!" cried a stern voice in the room, "you who have no more discretion than thus to talk with the dead."

The old man arose and stood up; his keen eyes dwelt firmly upon Ross, and with his right hand he drew the covering from the dead. There was something noble in the look and attitude of that gray-headed negro as he confronted the false friend, the household traitor, who might yet have almost the power of life and death over him.

"He is my master; I will not leave him," said the old man firmly. "You may whip me, you may kill me, but I will never leave him till he is buried. I rocked him in his cradle; I will lay him in his grave. Then sell me, if you like; no matter what becomes of the old man when his master is in the grave." And turning away with a look of unutterable woe, the old servant cast himself by the death-couch, crying out, "My master! oh, my master!"

A few weeks after, the old man was sold and sent away to a far-off plantation, for he was a part of the property which Daniel Clark had left, and according to the old will, the only one ever found, Ross was the executor of the estate and had a right to sell the poor old man.

CHAPTER FIVE

YOUTHFUL DREAMS

A being o' beauty she fell to her dreaming—
Thought flitted in gleamings of light through her brain,
In the depths of her eye it was constantly gleaming,
Still lighting her soul with soft visions again.

The will of Daniel Clark was never found, and the vast inheritance that should have been his child's became the spoil of those who had crept like vipers along his life-path, poisoning every pure blossom that sprang up to bless him on his way to the grave. His wife was bereft of everything but her sorrowful memories. His child had not even these. To her, father, mother, all was a dream—an idea that had floated through her infant memory and was gone.

Years went by—many years—and then in one of the most splendid mansions of Philadelphia, lay a fair young girl, half arrayed in her morning costume, and but partially aroused from one of those sweet dreams that of late had made her sleep a vision of love. While lifting the wealth of her brown hair between both her small hands in dressing before her mirror that morning, she had been taken with one of those rich gleams of thought that are the poetry of youth, and allowing the tresses to fall over her slight person again, where, in their wonderful and bright abundance, they fell almost to her feet, she had stolen thoughtfully to a couch in her boudoir and cast herself upon the crimson cushions. There, with some loose drapery gathered around her, one fair cheek resting in the palm of her hand, and the white arm half vailed by those loosened tresses, pressed deep in the silken cushions, the young girl fell into a reverie. Perhaps the dream from which she had just been aroused still haunted her mind, but it would have been difficult for Myra herself to have said what were the strange and sweet fancies that floated through her mind at that moment; for her own thoughts were a mystery, her feelings vague as they were pure. These sort of day-dreams, when they come to our first youth, have much of heaven in them; if they could only endure through life always bright, always enveloped in the same rosy mist,

> *Man might forget to dream of heaven,*
> *And yet have the sweet sin forgiven.*

Myra was aroused from her day-dream, not rudely as some of our sweetest fancies are broken, but by a light footfall, and a soft voice that called her name from the inner room. The young girl started up—

"Mother—mother, is it you—am I very late this morning?"

"Oh, you are here, daughter," said a middle-aged and gentle lady as she entered the boudoir. "No, not very late, but do you know that your father has just arrived and is inquiring for you?"

"My father here, and I not half ready to go down!" cried Myra, eagerly gathering up her hair, while, with the wonderful mobility natural to her features, the whole tone of her face changed. The dreamy, almost languid expression vanished in an instant. The warm glow of her affectionate nature broke through every feature like flame hidden in the heart of a pearl. Her cheek, her mouth, her white forehead were full of animation; her brown eyes sparkled with delight. With her whole being she loved the man whom she believed to be her father, and for the gentle woman who stood gazing upon her with so much affection as her toilet was completed, Myra's devotion was almost more than the natural love of a child for its mother. Scarcely a minute elapsed before the young girl was ready to go down. Another minute and she was in the arms of a fine and noble-looking man who stood by the breakfast-room door eagerly watching for her. During many weeks he had been absent from his home, and he could not feel thoroughly welcomed back again while Myra was not by to greet him.

It was a joyous family party that gathered around the breakfast-table that morning. The eyes of that gentle wife wandered, with a look of grateful affection, from the noble face of her husband to meet the sparkling glance of her child; for Myra was more than a child to her. Rejoiced to be once more in the bosom of his family, Mr. D. was more than usually animated and agreeable. There was not a hidden thought or a disunited feeling in the little family group.

"And whom have you had to visit you since I went away, Myra? What new conquest have you made? Tell me all about it, child," said Mr. D., smiling, as he received the coffee-cup of Sevres china from the hands of his wife.

Myra laughed—a clear, ringing laugh that had more of hearty glee in it than any thing you ever heard.

"Oh, we have had crowds of visitors, gallants without number. Ladies like a swarm of humming-birds, and—and—oh, yes; we had one very singular and romantic person, a namesake and intimate friend of yours, papa. I wrote you about him, but you never mentioned him at all in your reply."

"Oh, yes; I remember," said Mr. D., "a grave, gentlemanly old man, with just gray hairs enough to make him interesting, and the most winning manners. He carried a little Bible with a gold clasp in his bosom—I remember the description well. What of him, Myra? You lost your heart, of that the letter told me—but who was this mysterious person? Pray, enlighten me."

Myra and her mother exchanged glances. A faint crimson broke over the elder lady's face, and the young girl looked a little puzzled.

"Why, papa, how strangely you talk. This gentleman knows you well; he is a member of the legislature, and his seat is close by yours in the house," said Myra.

"Nonsense, child; there is but one man of my name in the house, and he has not been absent from Harrisburg a day during the session; besides, he has not a white hair in his head, and never carries small Bibles with gold clasps to exhibit to young ladies. You have had some impostor here. What did the interesting gentleman want?"

"He had lost a portmanteau that contained his money and clothes," faltered Myra.

"All but the little Bible!" cried her father with a laugh.

"And so," continued the young girl, blushing, "as he was a friend of yours and out of money, he only desired mamma to advance him a small sum."

"And she did it—I'll be sworn she did it!" cried Mr. D. enjoying the blushes of his wife. "The scoundrel carried off my wife's purse and my daughter's heart at one fell swoop."

"It was not much, only twenty-four dollars," said the lady struggling to bear up against her husband's raillery.

"But I—I told him he could have fifty just as well," said Myra, joining in her father's laugh. "Who could suspect him with his gentle manners—"

"And little Bible?" interrupted Mr. D.

"And gray hairs? Indeed, papa, it was worth the money to be cheated so gracefully. You have no idea with what an air the man took his leave—the tears absolutely stood in his eyes."

"The fellow was a fool not to take your fifty dollars, Myra, that is all I have to say about him—so now on with your list. What other interesting stranger have you entertained in my absence?"

Myra hesitated, her eyes drooped for an instant, and the damask of her cheek deepened to crimson. For the first time in her life she felt embarrassed in the presence of her father. What if papa should pronounce *him* an impostor also? she thought; and her heart was in a glow at the very idea. She felt that the eyes of her father were fixed on her inquiringly, and this deepened her confusion.

"We have received one other stranger here," she said at length, making an effort to look up, "a very talented and agreeable gentleman, whom I met by accident when out on an excursion."

"Indeed; and who is he?" inquired Mr. D. in a grave tone, and casting a glance at his wife that had a shade of displeasure in it.

"He seems a most estimable young man, full of talent and generous feeling," said Mrs. D., anxious to save her child from the embarrassment of an answer.

"He *seems*—who is he?" demanded the husband; his voice was stern and his look suspicious. "Myra, who is this man?"

"His name is Whitney," replied the young girl, resuming something of her natural courage. "I have made no further inquiries; but he is no impostor, papa, I am very sure of that."

Mr. D. arose from the table, evidently much annoyed. Myra's heart beat quick. Why should she tremble, why should every nerve in her slight frame thrill so, if the stranger were no more to her than a hundred others had been? Why was it that the laugh died on her lip, and all her courage fled, when she saw the displeasure so strongly marked in her father's face? Was the young girl awaking from her dream? Did she begin to feel how truly, how ardently she loved? or was the rosy vail but half lifted from her heart? She cast a supplicating glance at her mother, and her look was answered by one of sweet and undisturbed affection. That feminine and lovely woman could sympathize far better with the sweet, wild feelings that broke so eloquently, that moment, through the troubled eyes of her child, than with the stern displeasure of her husband. She arose from the breakfast-table and glided from the room, making a sign for her daughter to follow.

"Stay," said the master of the house, addressing Myra, as she was turning toward her own room. "I would ask a single question, and then let us have done with this impostor; for, doubtless, he is such."

"No, father, no; I would pledge my life for his honor. He is no impostor," exclaimed Myra, as her father led the way to a little study that opened from the breakfast-room.

"As you would have done for the gentlemanly old man with the Bible, I dare say," was the half-humorous, half-ironical rejoinder. "But answer my question, Myra: has this young man ever presumed to lift his eyes to you as an equal? Has he ever uttered a word that might lead you to suppose that he thinks of you save as a stranger?"

"Indeed, papa, he never has—far, far from it. When other young men have overwhelmed me with flatteries; when, as your heiress, homage of every kind has been lavished upon me, he alone has been silent. Always respectful, always kind, he has never, for one moment, taken the attitude often assumed by other young men who could not boast a tithe of his merit. He has seldom spoken to me of himself— never has the word love passed between us."

"You are eloquent, Myra, alike in the praise and in the defense of this stranger."

"I speak but the truth, papa."

"Well, I am glad of it. The whole affair can be more readily dismissed than I supposed. Now go to your chamber and think no more about it."

"Think no more about it;" truly it was a request easily made, but how impossible to obey. Why, the very thought of that stranger youth had henceforth the power of an angel which might steal down and trouble the still waters of her heart forever. Myra knew not even yet that this spirit took the form of love. She entered her boudoir again and flung herself upon the couch, but how changed were her feelings—the sweet dream, so tranquil, so full of rosy content, was swept away like a cloud. Her heart was in a tumult, her cheek burned, her eyes filled with tears. She felt indignant that her father should, for one moment, hold a doubt of the being in whom she put such perfect trust.

Thus musing with herself, the young girl spent an hour of disquiet, when her reverie was disturbed by a servant, who informed her that Mr. Whitney was in the drawing-room. Her first sensation was a thrill of joy, such as had long, unconsciously, followed his approach. The next was a feeling of reserve, a shy, half distrustful sensation, such as had never possessed her warm, frank nature before. She went down, not, as had been her wont, with the step of a gazelle, and with a glad smile sparkling in her eyes and on her lip, but with a lingering tread and eyes vailed by their snowy lids and dark lashes. She entered the drawing-room so gently that its occupant did not at first observe her. He stood by a marble table, near the window, turning over some books that lay upon it. The light which fell over him was subdued by many a glowing fold of damask that swept over the windows, thus giving the dim look of marble to features so perfectly classical in their outline, that but for that thick waving hair, and the glow of life that pervaded them, the head might have been taken for that of some antique statue. To these manly attractions were added a figure, tall beyond the ordinary standard, sinewy, athletic, and yet full of subtle grace.

While he thought himself alone a look of tranquil repose lay upon young Whitney's features, but the moment he lifted his head and saw the fair girl who stood hesitating by the door, the whole character of his face changed; a glow of animation lighted up his face, and he came forward with all the eager cordiality that her previous frank bearing had always warranted.

Myra hesitated before she reached forth her hand, and when she did place it in his, it quivered like an aspen. The young man looked earnestly in her changing face, and then led her to a seat, himself a prey to all the quick apprehension that her unusual restraint was calculated to inspire. A few common-place words were spoken, then both became silent and preoccupied. At length Myra observed that her father had returned home that morning, but she blushed while saying it, as if the young man could have guessed at the conversation that had given so much pain to herself.

A vague idea of the truth did evidently flash across the young man's mind, for he turned another long and earnest look upon her face, which was now glowing crimson to her temples, and when he turned his eyes away, the faintest possible smile stole over his lips.

"It is——" he said, with a faint sigh, "it is now more than two months since I arrived in Philadelphia. All that time your kind mamma has received me as a guest. Perhaps I should not have accepted this hospitality without first convincing her that I was not unworthy of it; but I found it so sweet to be taken on trust, so flattering to be valued for myself alone, that I had almost forgotten the reasonable demands of society. I ought long since to have convinced her that it was no impostor to whom her kindness had been extended."

"Impostor!" exclaimed Myra, with a smile that told how impossible she thought it that even suspicion should be attached to him.

"What if I were to be suspected as such?" added Whitney with an answering smile.

"I would not believe it—I would believe no wrong of you, though your own lips asserted it!" was the generous reply.

The color swept over young Whitney's face, and there was something in his eyes that deepened the crimson on Myra's cheek; but he only answered in a low and earnest voice:

"I thank you; with my whole heart I thank you for this confidence."

Then, after a moment's hesitation, he took from his pocket several letters which, with a hand that trembled somewhat, he presented to the young girl. She took them to the window, and, half shaded by the curtains, began to read, rejoicing in the obscurity, for she felt a terror that the quick beating of her heart might become visible.

The letters were from several of the first men in America—men whose autographs had become familiar to Myra upon the public records of the land. Nothing could have been more ample than the testimonials that these men gave of the high worth, talent, and position sustained by young Whitney.

Myra read these letters with a feeling of proud triumph. Her trust in him was sustained; she had never distrusted his worth, and in her hand she held the proud power of crushing every doubt that her father might have had. Merit to which the highest and purest in the land bore such testimony could never again become subject of dispute. She returned to Mr. Whitney. The generous enthusiasm that wholly possessed her beamed in every lineament of a face lovely in itself, but most remarkable for a quick and brilliant expression seldom equaled in the human countenance.

"Mr. Whitney, may I retain these only a short time? My father—he will be pleased to see them."

Myra was petite and slight in her person, almost as a fairy. As she stood clasping the letters between her hands, and with her eyes uplifted toward him, those eyes, so brilliant with every feeling of the heart, a prettier contrast with his tall and stately form could not well be imagined.

"Certainly; do with them as you please," he said; "but you must not allow your father to suppose that I exhibit them from ostentation."

"Oh, he will not think that!" cried Myra, extending her hand, for her guest was about to take his leave. "He will never think anything that is not noble and good of you, I am sure."

"Tomorrow, then—tomorrow I will call for the letters."

"Yes, tomorrow," replied Myra; and while a servant opened the door for her guest, she entered her father's study.

Mr. D. was seated by his escritoire, reading some papers. He looked up as Myra entered, and smiled kindly upon her.

"What visitor have you had?" he inquired, folding up the paper in his hand. "Did I not hear someone go out a moment since?"

"Yes, sir; it was Mr. Whitney."

Mr. D. tossed the paper he held upon the escritoire, and his brow contracted.

"Mr. Whitney again! Have I not told you, Myra, that no man of whose character I am not well informed shall visit my house? How can you thus receive a person of whom you know nothing?"

"But, papa, I do know all about him, now, and so may you. Only read these letters, and you will find that his family is as good as ours; his character irreproachable; his position every thing that can warrant the acquaintance he has sought."

Mr. D. took the letters very coldly, and without another word proceeded to read them. Myra watched his countenance with a palpitating heart. The frown remained immovable on his forehead, and his mouth relaxed nothing of its stern expression. Coldly and deliberately he read the letters through; laid them down one by one, and then placing his hand upon the parcel, turned to his daughter.

"What proof have we that these are not forgeries?" he said.

Myra's heart swelled indignantly. She could hardly force herself to answer. It seemed as if her father had determined to receive no evidence in favor of the man, against whom he had taken a prejudice that, to her warm nature, seemed most unjust and causeless.

"The handwriting, the autographs, are they not genuine? are they not sufficient?"

Mr. D. took up one of the letters and examined it closely. "The letters may be genuine; but what proof have we that this young man came by them honorably—in short, that his name is Whitney, or that he is at all the person for whom he represents himself?"

"Oh, papa, this is too much! Only see this young gentleman yourself, and then judge if he can be suspected of obtaining those letters by dishonorable means!"

Myra grew pale, and tears started to her eyes as she spoke. Mr. D. regarded her for a moment, then placing the letters in his escritoire, he turned the key. Myra waited for some answer to her appeal, but he coldly took up the paper that he had been reading as she came in, and seemed to cast the subject of conversation from his mind. Myra went to her chamber with a heavy heart; she felt chilled and hurt by her father's coldness: perhaps, too, there was in her heart a feeling of disappointment regarding Whitney also. In the slight mystery that had, up to that day, enveloped him, her ardent fancy had found something for the imagination to dwell upon. In the generosity of her youth she had rather hoped that he might prove one of those rare geniuses that struggle from an obscure origin and through poverty to the intellectual and moral eminence which alone she prized, and which she was certain he had attained. Perhaps some vague fancy of relieving his poverty by the wealth which, as her father's heiress, she must one day possess, had formed part of the day-dreams which of late had haunted her. Certain it is that a sensation of regret mingled with the sadness that her father's settled disapprobation had cast upon her spirits. She felt almost grieved by the proof that, even as a friend—for she had not allowed her thoughts to range beyond that gentle character—Whitney, from his worldly position, would never require a sacrifice from her.

The next day Whitney called again—called to take leave. He was about returning to his native State, and had only a moment in which to utter thanks and farewell to the friends whose kindness he should never cease to remember with gratitude. In a few months—it might be weeks—he would again visit Philadelphia, and to renew the acquaintance he had made would be one of his sweetest hopes till then.

Myra heard all this with that quiet and gentle dignity which no surprise could wholly conquer. She saw that her guest was agitated, that he was not taking leave of her with the indifference of a common acquaintance; and with that deep trust which true affection gives to the heart, her thoughts turned to the future. A few broken sentences passed between them, and then Myra went to her father for the letters that he had locked in his escritoire the day before.

"I will bring the letters myself," was the cold reply which was given to her request, and Myra returned to the drawing room pale and agitated, for there was something in her father's manner that filled her with vague apprehension.

A few moments elapsed, and then measured footsteps in the hall made the young girl's heart beat quick as she listened. They approached the drawing-room door; it was opened, and with a cold and stately politeness Mr. D. entered, holding the letters in his hand.

He approached Mr. Whitney, who had risen to receive him, and now resumed his seat. "Sir," he said, gravely drawing a chair and seating himself opposite to the young man, "there are the letters with which you have honored me; they are perfectly satisfactory."

There was something so chill and cutting in the measured tones and unbending courtesy with which this was said, that it had all the effect of an insult without yielding an excuse for resentment.

Whitney took the letters, and the color mounted to his temples. "I trust," he said, "that there was nothing in the letters, or in the manner of presenting them, that could give offense?"

Before answering, Mr. D. turned his eyes upon Myra, who sat pale and dismayed in a corner of the sofa, and made a motion of the head that she should leave the room.

The young girl arose trembling in every limb, and left the room; but while she stood upon the threshold struggling for strength to move on, her father spoke. "May I ask you, sir, why those letters were presented to my daughter?"

Whitney's voice was low but firm, as he answered:

"I have received much kindness from your family, sir, within the last two months, and could not leave the city, as I am about to do, without giving Mrs. D. and your daughter all the proof in my power that their hospitality had not been unworthily bestowed."

"And was this your only motive, sir?"

"It was my only motive."

"And have you not presumed to place yourself on an equality with my daughter? Have you not taken advantage of her youth and my absence to ingratiate yourself in her favor? In short, sir, have you not presumed upon the hospitality awarded by my wife, and offered address to my child, every way distasteful to her family?"

"No, sir, no, I have not thus presumed."

Myra heard no more—a sharp sense of humiliation, a thousand confused thoughts flashed through her brain, and with a pang at her heart such as she had never dreamed of before, she darted up the stairs.

White and gasping for breath, she paused at the top, made a grasp at the baluster for support, and, for the first time in her life, fainted upon the floor.

Humiliating and bitter, indeed, were the thoughts that flowed through the young girl's mind, when she awoke from her swoon and found the sweet face of her mother bending over her; proud and keenly sensitive, she felt as if the dignity of her self-respect had been irretrievably outraged. Never in his life had young Whitney spoken to her of love, and in all her thoughts of him, the idea of passion had never once mingled. But now she felt in her innermost heart that something stronger and more powerful than mere friendship had driven the blood from her heart when she heard him so cruelly arraigned for feelings and hopes that he had never breathed, perhaps had never felt. This knowledge of her own heart, thrust so rudely on the young girl, was but another pang added to her outraged pride, and for days not even the sweet and soothing care of her mother had power to console her.

In this state of feeling, Mr. D. left his child and returned to his legislative duties. The very day after his departure from home, there came a letter for Myra—a letter from the man who now occupied her every thought. She broke the seal in the presence of her mother, and read such words as made her heart thrill and her pale cheek glow again.

"Nothing but the harsh words of your father would have given me confidence to address you so," the letter said, "but there was something in those words, cruel and cold as they were, that gave me the first gleam of hope I have dared to entertain—hope that the great love I feel for you might be returned. Say only that this hope—it is faint and humble—will not be thought presumptuous, and surely some means can be found by which the prejudice which your father exhibits against me will be removed."

She loved, she was beloved. The weight that had bowed down her pride was swept away by that letter, like mists before a glowing sun.

A hopeful and joyous creature was Myra, and her light heart shook off the trouble that had oppressed it as a wild blossom casts the dew from its petals. She answered the letter. Modestly and with sensitive reserve, she vailed the affection that thrilled at her heart as she wrote to him for the first time, but still Myra answered her lover's first letter, and in all this her confidant was that loving and gentle mother.

"Let us hope for the best, my child," the fond woman would say. "When your father knows his worth as we do, and is satisfied that you love him truly, then he will relent. We have but to wait."

They did wait, and in the mean time letter after letter came and went, thus linking those two young hearts more and more firmly together.

Mr. D. came home at length, and now the true reason of his dislike to Whitney became manifest. Myra was intended for another. Wealth and station, everything that could win the sanction of a proud man, was in favor of her father's choice, and on the very day of his return he explained his intentions and his wishes to the young girl.

"You shall have a noble fortune, my child," he said. "Few ladies in America shall give so fine a property to a husband."

"Father!—" answered Myra, and it was wonderful how mild and firm the young girl remained, knowing, as she did, how powerful were the interests she opposed, with her fragile strength, "Father, I can not marry this man. I do not love him, and will never commit the sin of wedding without affection."

The young girl was very pale, but there was a mild firmness in her eye that revealed all the pure strength that sustained her. She paused, drew a deep breath, and while her father stood gazing upon her, dumb with astonishment, she added:

"I will never marry any man but Mr. Whitney, for while he lives I can never love another."

And now that it was over, Myra began to tremble; for there was something terrible in the fierce and pallid rage that held her father for a time mute and motionless before her. At length his lips parted, and his eyes flashed.

"Whitney! the ingrate, the impostor, you love!—you would marry him against my consent?"

"No, I will never marry any man against your consent, papa," replied Myra, bursting into tears; for her strength had been taxed to the utmost, and she was not one to brave a parent's wrath unmoved. "I can remain single, and will, if you desire it; but with the feelings that I have for Mr. Whitney, it would be a sin should I give one thought to another."

Mr. D. gazed on the pale, earnest face of his child as she spoke, but there was no relenting in his face. Anger, scorn, a thousand wrathful passions broke through its pallor, and he answered in a voice of cutting scorn:

"And this man, you told me, had never breathed a word of love to you in his life."

Myra was about to acknowledge the letters that had passed between Whitney and herself, for there was a seeming justice in the proud man's taunt that cut her to the heart; but she thought of her mother, of the self-sacrificing mother who had so generously risked the displeasure of her husband in sanctioning the letters her child had received, and she only answered, "I can never love another, papa."

Mr. D. turned away, and began to pace the room. His lips were pressed forcibly together, and uncontrollable passion seemed burning in every vein of his body.

"Thank God!—" he muttered, turning furiously upon the terrified girl, "Thank God, no drop of *my* blood runs in your veins."

"Papa! O papa! this is terrible. Why, in your anger against me, say things that are so cruel as they are without foundation?" cried Myra, starting to her feet, and approaching her father.

"Without foundation! It is true, girl, I say it is true you are not my child!"

She did not believe him. How could she, poor girl; with the household links of many a happy year clinging about her heart? One word could not tear them away so readily, but the very thought made her pale as a corpse, and every nerve of her delicate frame trembled. A reproachful smile quivered over his lips, and she laid her hand upon the stern man's arm.

"O father! I know that you are only angry; but this is too much. It would kill me to hear you say that again."

Mr. D. turned. Anger was fierce within him still, and he took no pity on that pale and tortured girl.

"As there is a heaven above, you are not my child! I can prove it—have the papers in the house that you shall see."

A faint cry burst from Myra's lips. She staggered back and fell upon a chair, her eyes distended, and fixed wildly upon the stern man, as if she searched in those angry features for a contradiction of the words he had spoken. She saw nothing there to relieve the doubt that ached at her heart.

"Not my father? mamma not my mother?" she murmured, and the tears began to rain over her white cheeks. She suddenly clasped her hands and stood up.

"Then whose child am I?"

Mr. D. sat down; the angry fire was fast going out from his heart, and it could sustain him no longer. Regret, keen and self-accusing, took possession of him then. Love, pity, every tender feeling that had so long enlinked that young girl to his heart, all came back like birds to a ravaged nest. He would have given worlds for the power to annihilate those ten minutes of his life, when one fierce gleam of anger had unlocked the hoarded secret of years. He turned his eyes almost imploringly on the trembling girl. His proud lip quivered, his hand shook as he rested it on his knee. Myra crept toward him, heart-broken and wretched, beyond all her previous ideas of wretchedness. She laid her hand upon his shoulder, and bent her face to his as she had done many a time in her childhood, when some small trouble oppressed her. But oh! how unlike her sweet childhood were those agonized features?

"Father—father!" she said, and her voice bespoke it its low and thrilling tones all the anguish he had inflicted. "Father, tell me, whose child am I?"

"To-morrow, to-morrow!" said Mr. D.; "I can go through no more to-day."

"But is it true that I am not your child?" said Myra, still hoping against hope.

"It is true!" he answered; and, rising from his seat with an unsteady step, he entered his study.

A moment after, Mrs. D. met Myra on the stairs. One glance in her face was enough. "Myra, daughter!" she exclaimed, "What is this? You are white as death—you tremble."

"Mother—mother!" burst from the lips of the young girl, almost with a shriek. "They tell me that I am not your child!"

Mrs. D. was struck motionless. Marble could not have been more coldly white than her face and hands.

"And who—who has told you this?" she faltered.

"He told me himself—papa—he has the proofs. Mother, mother, say in mercy that he is only angry—that it is not so!"

With a wild gesture, and a burst of passionate tears, the unhappy girl cast herself into her mother's arms. The poor lady trembled beneath the weight of that fragile form. She wove her arms around it; she pressed kiss after kiss upon that forehead with her cold and quivering lips. She strove, by the warmth and passion of her maternal love, to charm away the pain and the truth from her daughter's heart, but she said not in words, "Myra, you are my child," and the young girl arose from her bosom utterly desolate.

The morrow came, and Myra stood by her father in his study, for he was still a father to her. The escritoire was open before them, and a large pocket-book, with the seal wrenched apart, lay upon the lid. Mr. D. sat with his head bent and shading his troubled forehead with one hand. Myra held a letter in her shaking grasp—a letter addressed to the man whom she had always deemed her parent, and signed by Daniel

Clark. She could not read; the words swam before her eyes, but she laid her finger on the signature and said in a low and husky voice, "This name—Daniel Clark—he was my godfather."

"He was your father!" replied Mr. D. "Read, read for yourself."

Myra forced her nerves to be still. With desperate resolution she kept her eyes upon the writing. Every word of that letter contained proof that went to her heart. She was the daughter of Daniel Clark.

CHAPTER SIX

THE TRUTH REVEALED

She left the parent roof, and left in grief,
Not from an idle passion vain and light,
But in her heart there lived a firm belief,
That duty call'd and honor urged her flight.

Little by little, as her shattered nerves could bear it, the truth was revealed to Myra. It was a sad, sad trial, the uprooting of her pure domestic faith, the tearing asunder of those thousand delicate fibers that had so long woven, and clung and rooted themselves around the parents who had adopted her. Love them she did, now, as it seemed, more intensely than ever, but there was excitement in her heart, a sort of wild, unsettled feeling, that destroyed all the sweet faith and tranquility of affection. It was no longer the quiet and serene love which had clung around her from infancy, naturally and without effort, as wild blossoms bud upon a bank where the sunshine sleeps longest—but something of unrest and pain mingled with it all. In the history of her parents she found much to excite her imagination, her deep and sorrowful interest. It opened upon her with all the vividness of a romance, that kindled her fancy, while it pained her to the soul.

Then came other thoughts and more thrilling anxieties. The beloved one, the man of her choice, whom she had dreamed of endowing with riches, from which she now seemed legal dispossessed—how would he receive the news of her orphanage—of her dependent state? Alas, how were all her proud and generous visions swept away! And yet, did she doubt his love or his pure disinterestedness? Never for a moment. Loyal, lofty, and unselfish as her own pure heart, she knew the beloved of that heart to be. She felt assured that his faith to the dowerless orphan would be kept more sacred than his pledge to the heiress. Full of this high trust, she wrote to Whitney and told him the whole.

"You sought me," said the letter, "and loved me as the heiress of great wealth, as the only daughter of a proud and rich man. All at once, as if a flash of lightning had swept across the horizon of my life, revealing the truth with a single fiery gleam, I find myself the orphan of a great and good man, whom I remember only as the shade of a vision—and of a woman, lovely as she has been unfortunate—alive still, but kept from her child by bonds that have yet proved too strong, even for the yearnings of maternal love. I know that Daniel Clark, my father, was supposed to possess great wealth, but I am told that he died insolvent, and that in his will neither wife nor child was mentioned. Therefore am I an orphan, dependent upon those who are strangers to me in blood for the love that shelters me, for the wealth that has hedged me in with comforts from my cradle up. ★ ★ ★ ★ ★ ★ ★ I am not the person whom you loved—not the person whom, two short days ago, I believed myself to be. Should Myra Clark, orphaned and without inheritance—her very birth loaded with doubt, and her hold on any living thing uncertain—still claim the faith pledged to Myra D., the heiress? No; like the rest, I resign this last and most precious hold on the past. You are free—honorably free, from all responsibility arising from the faith you plighted. Of all my past life, I have nothing left but the simple name of Myra."

This is but an extract of Myra's letter to Mr. Whitney, but it was enough to satisfy her delicate sense of honor. It set him free. It relinquished all claim upon his faith or his honor. Much there was in the letter to melt and touch a heart like his, for with a great secret swelling in her breast, she found consolation in pouring out the feelings that oppressed her, where she was certain of sympathy.

And Whitney answered the letter. He had not loved the heiress or the lofty name—but Myra, the noble-minded, the lovely, the beautiful. If she was an orphan, so much the better; he would be family, wealth, the world to her. He grieved for her sorrow, but seemed to revel and rejoice in the idea of having her all to himself. This was the tenor of Whitney's reply, and Myra felt no longer alone—her elastic nature gathered up its strength again. She became proud of the pure and holy love, which only grew brighter with adversity, and this beautiful pride rekindled all her energies.

Among the fine scenery which lies upon the upper portions of the Delaware Bay, there is a splendid old mansion-house, large, massive, and bearing deeper marks of antiquity and aristocratic ownership, than are usually found in a country where dwellings that have withstood the ravages of a hundred years are seldom to be found. It was a superb country place, uplifted above the bay, and commanding one of the finest prospects in the whole country. Picturesque and broken scenery lay all around. Portions of this scenery were wild, and even rude, in their thrifty luxuriance, while close around the dwelling reigned the most perfect cultivation. Park-like groves, lawns fringed with choice shrubberies, and glowing with a profusion of flowers, might be seen from every window of the dwelling. The stables, lodges, and other buildings, all in excellent repair, bespoke a degree of prosperous wealth, and a luxurious taste, seldom found in our primitive land. A spacious veranda that ran along the front, commanded a beautiful view of the distant bay and all the broken shore, for miles and miles on either hand. In the whole State of Delaware could not have been found, at that day, a gentleman's residence more perfect in itself, or more luxurious in its appointments. To this house Mr. D. took his family to spend the summer months, and Myra entered it, for the first time in her life, with a feeling of profound loneliness. This noble mansion was to have been her inheritance. She had spent all her girlhood in the shadows of its walks; she had learned to love every tree and flower and shady nook that surrounded it—to love them as the home of her parents, the home that should hereafter shelter her and her children. Now she entered it sadly, and with a feeling of cold desolation. Transient, certainly, but very painful were these natural regrets.

But amid all the shadows that hung around her path, there was one gleam of golden sunshine. *His* love was left to her—*his* faith still remained firm and perfect.

With the visitors who came with Mr. D. to his country dwelling, was a distant relation of the family, his wife, and two lovely children. To these persons the secret of Myra's birth was made known, and to the lady, young and apparently amiable, Myra sometimes fled for counsel and sympathy. But to these persons the secret of Myra's parentage opened new and selfish hopes that forbade all genuine friendship for the confiding girl. Myra, severed by all ties of blood from the family that had adopted her, now seemed only an obstacle in the way of their own interests. The excessive love still expressed for her both by Mr. D. and his angelic wife, seemed so much defrauded from the rights of their own offspring, and those who had flattered and fawned abjectly on the daughter and the heiress now returned the touching confidence of the orphan with treachery and dislike.

Thus surrounded by secret enemies and those sad regrets which hopes so suddenly crushed could not fail to excite, the young girl yielded her whole being up to the one sweet hope still left to her, undimmed and brightening each day—a lone star in the clouded sky of her life. The love, that under other circumstances might have been diversified by many worldly fancies, now concentrated itself around her whole being, and in its pure intensity became almost sublime.

Mr. D. in revealing the secret of Myra's birth had, as it were, thrown off all claims to her filial obedience, but the generous girl took no advantage of this most painful freedom; her great desire was still to win his consent to her union with the man she loved, her penniless union, for Myra neither hoped nor wished for any thing more than the love of those who had protected her infancy to carry as a marriage dower to her husband. Under the sanction of her gentle mother—for such Mrs. D. was ever to Myra—the young girl had still carried on a correspondence with Mr. Whitney, and it was decided that he should write to Mr. D. and again request permission to visit the young creature, who, without a daughter's right, had no desire to evade a daughter's obedience.

Believing the acquaintance between Myra and her love broken off by his own firm opposition, Mr. D. had not given up her union with another, which had for many years been a favorite object with him. His astonishment and indignation may, therefore, be imagined, when the mild and respectful letter of Mr. Whitney reached him at D. Place, some few weeks after the retirement of his family to their country mansion. It was early in the morning when this letter came, and Mr. D. was alone with his relative and guest when he broke the seal. The anger that shook the proud man's nerves, the sharp exclamation that sprang from his lips, were heard by Mrs. D. as she passed into the breakfast-parlor. She saw the handwriting crushed angrily between the fingers of her husband, and filled with dread that Myra's private correspondence had been betrayed, she left the room and hastened to her daughter's chamber.

"O Myra! I fear—I fear that your papa has in some way obtained one of Mr. Whitney's letters," cried the generous lady, with a face that bespoke all the anxiety that preyed upon her.

Myra turned a little more pallid than usual, for her father's anger was a terrible thing to brave—of that she was well aware; but, after a moment, her natural courage returned, and she answered with some degree of firmness:

"Dear mamma, do not look so terrified. Let his anger fall on me; sit down. That pale face must not tell him that you have ever known of these letters."

Mrs. D. sank to a seat, striving to regain some degree of composure, and Myra went down-stairs, very pale, but making an effort to sustain with dignity the reproaches that she felt to be prepared for her.

"Here, young lady!" said Mr. D. as Myra entered the room; "Here is a letter from that Whitney again—a letter to me—asking permission to visit you."

Myra drew a deep breath; in her agitation she had forgotten that this letter might be expected, and so long as her father's anger had only this source, she could withstand it.

"Well, papa, and you will answer it?" said the young girl, gently, but still with some tremor of the voice.

"I will!" was the angry reply, "I will answer it as such presumption deserves!"

"Surely—surely, papa, you will not forget that Mr. Whitney is a gentleman, and deserving of courteous treatment?"

"I forget nothing!" was the curt reply; and without further argument Mr. D. left the room, and in half an hour after an old colored man was galloping toward Wlimington, with a letter, directed to Mr. Whitney, in his pocket. What that letter contained might have been guessed from the hasty and blotted address, had it not been written black as night on the angry forehead of Mr. D. when he sat down to breakfast that morning.

A few days went by—days of keen anxiety to poor Myra and her gentle mother; then was the young girl summoned once more to the presence of Mr. D. She found him white with rage—deeper and more terrible rage than his fine features had ever exhibited before. A letter was clenched tightly in his hand; his fingers worked convulsively around the crushed paper as he addressed the trembling girl.

"Twice—twice in my life have I been insulted, girl! By your father once—by your lover now. He is coming here! He will be in Wilmington in a few days, will he! Let him come; but as I live—as I live, girl, he shall never leave that place alive! This insult shall be atoned then and there."

"O father!" was all poor Myra could say.

"If he is a gentleman, he shall answer this *as* a gentleman. If he is what I suppose, then I will chastise this insolence as I would a menial. When once we meet, one or the other will never return alive."

Myra shuddered, her pale lips refused to utter the words that sprang to them, and she stood before the angry man with her hands clasped, but motionless as a statue. At length she gathered strength to utter a single sentence.

"Father, you will not challenge Mr. Whitney? It would be terrible; it would kill me."

"If he comes within my reach, if he dares to intrude his presence even into the neighborhood, he shall answer it with his life or mine!" was the stern reply.

Myra turned away trembling and heart-sick; she knew that this was no idle threat, no mere burst of vivid passion that would die within the hour. Her lover would be in Wilmington in a few days; it was a firm but courteous announcement to this effect that had so exasperated the man whom she had just left.

"Mother—mother, he will not do this thing—he will not meet Mr. Whitney with a challenge!" cried the harassed young creature, throwing herself into the arms of Mrs. D., who stood in the chamber of her child, where she had retired from the angry storm below.

"I fear it, alas! He deems himself braved and insulted," said the good lady, weeping bitterly. "O Myra! Why did we permit Whitney to write—why consent to his coming to the neighborhood?"

"Why, why, indeed! If it is but to meet his death?" cried the poor girl, wringing her hands. "But, mother, this can not be; my father will relent!"

Mrs. D. shook her head. "Not where he deems his honor or authority contemned, my poor child!"

"Oh, what can we do—what can we do?"

"His anger is so terrible—if you could but give up all thoughts of the man; if you only could, my child."

Myra withdrew from her mother's arms, her slight form seemed to dilate and nerve itself for some great effort. The tears hung unshed upon her eyelashes, and her lips were pressed firmly together. The thoughts that swept across her sweet face were quick and painful; she scarcely seemed to breathe, so intense was the struggle within that motionless bosom.

"Mother," she said, in a low and husky voice, so low that it was almost a whisper, "Mother, I will give him up. It is to save his life or the life of your husband; I will give him up!"

While the unhappy lady stood wondering at the strange calmness with which these words were spoken, Myra passed downstairs once more, and stood in her father's presence, calm, resolute, but very sorrowful.

"Father, I love the man whom you would challenge, whom you would force to the extremities of life or death. How dearly, how wholly I love him, you can never believe, or this agony would have been spared me. Father, you know of his coming; he is already on the way; thus it is out of my power to prevent that which so offends you. Let him come; let him depart in peace, and here I solemnly promise never to speak to him again. Father, I give him up, but it is to save his life or yours!"

The young girl ceased speaking; the words she had uttered were pronounced hurriedly and with firmness, but the white lips, the heavy trouble that clouded her eyes with something more touching than tears, revealed all the heroism of her sacrifice. You could see that to save a human life, she had given up all that made her own life valuable. It was strange to see so much heroism in a form so gentle and so frail; it was strange that this beautiful spirit of self-sacrifice should prove powerless to curb the wrathful spirit that possessed the proud man before whom she pleaded, but his answer was relentless.

"No!" he replied. "That which I have said is immutable! If this man comes so near my house as the next town, he shall answer for the presumption with his life, or I will sacrifice mine!"

Myra stood for a moment looking in that frowning face, and as she gazed her own became painfully calm.

"My father, once again—once again reflect, it is more than life that I offer you for this!" she said, and her voice grew softer, as if tears were swelling in its tones once more.

"That which I have said I abide by!" was the stern reply.

Myra pleaded no longer, but turned gently and left the room. In the upper hall she met her mother.

"Does he relent—will he accept the sacrifice of your offer?" questioned the anxious lady.

"No, mother, he refuses. He seems athirst for the life of this noble young man; but I will save him, I will save them both."

"How, my child? How can you, so frail and so helpless, struggle against the strong will of your father?"

"I will leave the house. I will no longer remain where innocent and honorable love leads to scenes like this."

"What, leave your mother—your own fond, too fond mother? Myra, my child, my child!"

"Hush! mother; dear, dear mother; these tears, they make me weak as an infant. If you weep and cling to me thus, mother, my strength may fail; and do you not know that death may follow—death to your husband or to mine, for is he not my husband before God, do you think, sweet mother?"

But Mrs. D. only wept, and clung more fondly to her daughter. Myra withdrew herself gently from that warm clasp, and went away. On the morrow Mr. Whitney would be in Wilmington, and before then the young girl had much to accomplish—much to suffer.

All that day Myra avoided the family, above all the gentle mother, whose tears she feared far more than the anger of her proud father. She had formed a resolution that required all her courage, and more strength than seemed to animate that slender form. She shrunk, therefore, from encountering the tears of that sweet and loving woman.

There was an old servant in the family, with whom Myra from her childhood had been a sort of idol. Indeed, in all that large household there was not a dependent who did not reverence and love the young creature. This man, early in the afternoon, might have been seen riding toward Wilmington at a brisk trot, and with some little anxiety in his manner. When he reached the town the old man entered a dwelling where he was received by two bright and joyous looking young ladies, who greeted him eagerly, and inquired for news of his young mistress, while the old negro was searching in his pockets for a hastily folded billet, which he, at length, produced with no little mysterious importance. One of the young ladies tore open the billet, and began to read.

Sit up for me to-night, dear girls, sit up till morning, unless I come before; you will certainly see me during the night; then I will explain this hasty message. It may storm; no matter, I shall surely be with you.

—MYRA.

The young ladies looked at each other, wholly at a loss to guess the reason of this singular message, but Myra had promised to explain all, and so they allowed the old man to depart unquestioned.

Long before the faithful messenger returned, Myra was standing in the humble dwelling of an out-door dependent in whom she could trust.

"And you are determined, Miss Myra," was the man's question as he stood, hat in hand, by the door.

"Yes; obey my directions exactly as they are given, that is all I require of you."

"We would do any thing—any thing on earth for you," said the wife of this man, coming forward. "You know we would, Miss Myra, even though it may be our ruin should your father know that we aided you against his will!"

"But he never can know; nothing shall tempt me to inform him, and the secret will rest with us alone," was the prompt reply.

"We will be punctual, never fear," said the man, "but it looks like a storm."

"Well," said Myra, casting her eyes toward the heavens, which did indeed bear indications of a mustering tempest, "it does not matter; be ready all the same. Remember to come by the old carriage route, not along the new road—you might meet company there."

"I will be cautious, dear young lady; I will be cautious as you could wish."

"I am sure of it," was the mild and grateful reply; and with a beating heart Myra went back to the house which was soon to be her home no longer.

The relation whom we have mentioned was still at D. Place, and his wife, with her two beautiful children, occupied a room near that appropriated to Myra, and to this room the young girl betook herself after returning from the visit to her humble friends. A spirit of unrest was upon her; she longed for action, for sympathy, for some being to whom she could pour forth the anguish which beat like a fever in every vein of her delicate body.

Myra found her father's guest in an easy chair near the window. She was a quiet, tranquil woman, devoid of strong passions, but selfish in the extreme, and possessing a sort of gentle craft that from its very want of active spirit was calculated to deceive. She knew that discontent and disunion were active in the dwelling, and after her usual inert manner was waiting for some result that might prove beneficial to herself and her children. When she saw Myra enter her room with a glow upon her cheek, but pale as death about the mouth and temples, this woman drooped her eyelids to conceal all expression of the joy this agitation kindled in her bosom, but her look was tranquil, her voice was full of sympathy as she addressed the young girl.

"You look anxious, nay, ill, my sweet friend," she said, taking Myra's hand, which fell over the back of her chair.

"You know," answered Myra, in a sad voice, "you know what has passed to-day in this house; tell me—for much depends on your answer, and I can hold counsel with no one else beneath this roof—tell me, do you believe that if Mr. Whitney should arrive in Wilmington to-morrow, my father would find him out and put his cruel threat into execution."

"You know Mr. D. Is he not determined? Did he ever swerve from a resolution once formed?" was the mild and sinister reply.

"Then you honestly believe that he would challenge Mr. Whitney?" was the anxious rejoinder.

"Has he not said it, Myra?"

"Then if you think so—you who always look on events so still and passionless—I have but to go on," said Myra, in accents that bespoke all the grief this conviction fastened on her young heart.

"What do you mean, Myra—what is it you contemplate?" said the confidant, with a gleam of satisfaction in her downcast eyes.

"I am going from this house to-night. Before Mr. Whitney reaches Wilmington, I will see him and prevent this meeting."

"You, Myra! you—what will your father say? What will the world think?"

"It is to save life!" answered Myra. "My own soul tells me that I am right."

The wily confidant dropped her head upon her hand, when she fell into a moment's thought. With all her apparent apathy, she knew well how to excite the resolution of a generous and ardent nature like Myra's, while seeming to oppose it. The arguments that she used appealed entirely to those selfish considerations which were sure to be cast away with disdain by the young creature on whom they were urged, and Myra went out from the interview more impressed than ever with the necessity of putting her project into immediate operation.

The storm that had been threatening all day came on at nightfall with all the rush and violence of a tempest, but this scene suited well with the excitement and wild wish for action which swelled in the young girl's heart, even as the elements heaved and struggled without. She sat by the window, gazing upon the storm; the trees tossing their branches to and fro like giants reveling in the wind; the rain sweeping downward in wreaths and sheets of silvery water whenever the lightning glared over it; and afar off the distant bay, heaving into sight, as it were, from the very bosom of darkness, and sinking back again when the lightning withdrew the sweep of its fiery wing.

Mr. D., full of unrest as the elements, was pacing the veranda—his face was unnaturally pale in the gleams of lightning, and he paced up and down, unconscious or heedless of the water-drifts that now and then swept over him. Poor Myra sat watching him; the storm within her own breast and the tempest without, imparted to her spirit a wild and reckless courage. She stepped out on the veranda; the rain beat in her pale face, the lightning glared across her eyes, already more than brilliant. She met her father in his walk, and touched his arm with her cold hand.

"Father, father! you have reflected. Oh, say that you will not provoke Mr. Whitney into this death-strife when he comes."

Mr. D. paused for one moment, a shade of irresolution swept across his features, but it left them more pale, more resolute than before; he turned away without a word of answer, and Myra disappeared.

That night, close upon the hour of twelve, two people, a man and a woman, stood near a back entrance of Mr. D.'s dwelling. The female held an umbrella, dripping and drenched with rain; the man stood with his ear bent to the door, listening.

At last, amid the storm, he heard a key turn and a bolt withdrawn; then the door swung open, and Myra appeared, wrapped in a large shawl, and standing by a little trunk which the slender girl had dragged step by step down the lofty staircase.

"Carry it carefully; there is neither lock nor key; it was the only one I could reach," she whispered, dragging her humble burden toward the man, who swung it to his shoulders and disappeared in the darkness.

Myra drew close to the woman, and sheltered by the dripping umbrella, followed after. A walk of some distance brought them to a carriage which stood waiting back of the stables; the steps were down, the horses and vehicle all drenched with rain, and furiously shaken by the wind, stood ready to receive her. She sprang, pale and breathless, into the frail shelter. Her faithful friend was about to mount the seat.

"One word," said Myra, bending her white face into the storm, "the turnpike gate—you may be known there if the man sees you. The storm rages so fiercely he may not be aroused, but if he is, make no answer; your voice, my good friend, would betray you, and this kindness to me might be your ruin with my father. If this man calls, do not speak; the gate is old, the horses good, the carriage strong; be resolute, and drive on as if nothing were in the way. Do you understand? Trample the old gate down, and that without a word. It will open your way back again."

"I will drive through the gate; never fear," was the prompt reply, and the man sprang to his seat.

One grateful shake of the hand, a smothered "God bless you, Miss Myra," from the good woman who had risked so much for her, and Myra fell back in the carriage.

The man was obliged to drive very slowly, for the night was intensely dark, and he only kept the road by the gleams of lightning that ever and anon flashed over it. At length they came to the turnpike gate that stretched its sodden timbers in a dark line across the road. The tempest was high, and every precaution was made to avoid the least noise, but the old toll-gatherer had a well-trained and most acute ear. Just as the driver was dismounting to try the lock of his gate, out came the old man, half-dressed, and with a candle in his hand that flared out the moment it felt a breath of the tempest.

"Halloa! Who goes there?" shouted the old fellow.

Myra leaned from the carriage: "Not a word—use the whip— down with the gate—but not a single word."

A firm sweep of the whip followed—a plunge—a crash—and then over the broken boards and through the black storm, the carriage was swept away. Along the dark road it toiled, pelted with rain, half-overturned every instant by a sweep of the wind, that kept rising stronger and higher, till on every hand rose the black, gaunt shadow of many a darkened dwelling, and in their midst a single light gleamed like a star.

"They are up—they are waiting!" exclaimed Myra, with a burst of grateful joy, as she saw this light. "Now, my friend—my good, kind friend—you must go no farther; even they must not see you. Stop here; set my trunk on the walk; I will find the way myself, now!"

The man would have protested against this, but Myra was firm, and there in that wild storm she stood till the carriage was out of sight. Then she seized the trunk by the handle, and straining every nerve in her delicate frame by the effort, dragged it toward a window where she saw two fair, young, beautiful faces peering anxiously out, as if they were searching for some loved object in the darkness.

All at once those faces disappeared, a sound of glad welcome came toward the door, and the next instant Myra, panting with fatigue, white as death, and drenched through and through, till the rain dripped like a rivulet from her garments, was folded in the arms of those noble-hearted girls.

CHAPTER SEVEN

TRUE FRIENDSHIP

Like a bird in the air,
Like a boat on the sea,
Like a fawn from its lair,
The maiden must flee.

While Myra was exchanging her drenched garments, and partaking of those refreshments which her late and comfortless ride rendered so necessary, she related to her young friends the cause of this sudden abandonment of her home; and they, with all the warm enthusiasm and vivid romance of youth, entered into her feelings and plans. There was no sleep for any of the pretty group that night, but closeted in a little bedroom, with a bright fire flashing and glowing over their lovely and eager faces, the young girls plotted and held council together, sometimes laughing at the miserable plight in which Myra had presented herself at the door; sometimes listening with a start, as if amid the rush and pause of the storm, they yet feared to detect the tread of some person in pursuit of the beautiful fugitive.

"And now," said Myra, after all had been told, "let us deliberate on the best step. At daylight I must start for New Castle, and thence to

Baltimore in time to prevent Mr. Whitney taking the boat. He must not approach Wilmington. Who will go with me? Where can I rest for a few hours in secrecy?"

"Who will go with you? why, father, of course," exclaimed one of the young girls, entering heart and soul into the interests of her friend. "Where can you rest? Have we not a brother married and settled at New Castle, who knows and loves you, even as we do? His wife will receive you, and joyfully enough."

Myra arose, her sweet face animated and sparkling with gratitude; she threw her arms around the young girl and kissed her.

"Oh, what friends you are; how I love you," she said, in her own frank, joyous way, turning to the other sister and pressing her forehead with lips that glowed with generous feeling. "It is worth while having a little trouble, if it were only to prove such hearts as yours. I shall never forget this night; never to my dying day."

"Oh, it is quite like a romance, Myra," exclaimed the younger of the girls, shaking back her ringlets, with a light laugh. "Here we had been for hours and hours watching at the window, with the rain beating and pelting on the glass close to our faces, and exactly like two characters in a novel. Then, between the flashes of lightning and the rain that absolutely came down in sheets—I never saw any thing like it in my life—you come toiling up to the door, like some poor little fairy shut out in the storm, your face so wet and pale, and your eyes floating like diamonds, and your black curls all dripping with rain. Upon my word, Myra, there was something unearthly about it all."

"Perhaps it was best," said Myra, smiling at the vivid fancy of her young friend. "Had the night been calm and every thing quiet, I should have felt it more. The storm gave me courage. It seemed as if the very rushing and outbreak of the elements excited a sort of heroism in my heart. Had it been a soft moonlight evening, when I could have seen the old trees, the flowers, and all those sweet objects that poor mamma and I have loved to look upon so often when the moonlight was on them, I could hardly have found strength to leave them all. Poor, poor mamma, how she will grieve; it will be a sad morning for her."

Myra bowed her head as she spoke, and her dark eyes filled with tears. The young girls gazed upon her with saddened countenances. This sorrow, so natural, so true, it was some thing to chill all their light ideas of romance.

Myra still sat with her face bowed down, lost in painful thought. Her heart was once more in its old home. She thought of the mother, the kind, gentle woman, who had taken her, like a young bird from the parent nest, and up to that very day had warmed her as it were with the pulses of her own heart into life and happiness. She thought of the proud old man, proud but full of strong affections; self-willed but generous; who was dignified and grand even in his error—of the old man who had loved her so long and so well. She thought of him, too, and the tears rolled fast and heavily down her cheeks. It was a terrible romance to her, poor thing. Nothing but a firm sense of right could have induced her to proceed a step further in it. She was no young heroine, but a noble, strong-minded woman, suffering keenly, but firm because she believed herself to be in the right. There was silence for a time, for the young girls respected the grief of their friend, then the eldest arose and leaning over Myra's chair, began with gentle delicacy to smooth and arrange the light tresses that had been so completely disordered by the storm.

"And when you have found Mr. Whitney, Myra, when you have prevented the meeting, how will it all end? In a wedding, and a reconciliation at the great house, no doubt," said the sweet girl, anxious to draw her friend from the painful reverie into which she had fallen.

"No," answered Myra, brushing the tears from her eyes, "I expect nothing like a reconciliation. When I abandoned D. Place last night, it was with no thoughts of return. I gave up every thing then."

"Every thing but love; every thing but the man who loves you," whispered her friend.

"Even love—even him—I gave up all. Do you think that I have a dream of marrying him now? That I intend to surround myself with the vulgar *eclat* of a 'runaway match?' It was to save his life that I left my home. I will meet him on the way, warn him of my father's hatred, and free him of all the engagements that have existed between us."

"And where will you go then, dear friend?"

"I have relatives in the West Indies, as I have been told, and I had resolved to seek their protection before leaving home."

"Then there will be no wedding after all, and we shall lose you altogether," cried the young girl, half in tears at the thoughts of this abrupt separation.

"Not forever; I am sure we shall meet again," answered Myra, casting an anxious glance through the window, for the conversation was arousing old feelings too keenly within her. "But it will soon be daylight."

"I have just aroused father, and told him all; he will go with you to New Castle," said the younger girl, who had been absent from the room. "The stage starts by daybreak."

Daybreak! The gray of morning was in the sky even then. Instantly there was a bustle of preparation in that little bedroom. Myra's garments, that had been drying by the fire, were hastily crowded into the trunk; a fathom or two was cut from the bed-cord, that her ill-secured luggage might have the best protection their means afforded, and at the appointed time all was ready for Myra's departure. Amid tears and affectionate embraces Myra parted with her young friends, and before the deep blue of night had fairly left the sky, she was on her route to New Castle.

The stage had no passengers except Myra and her kind attendant, so in the stillness of the morning she had nothing to distract her thoughts from the mournful channel into which they naturally turned. The storm had swept over the earth, leaving only freshness and beauty behind. The trees that bent over the road were vivid with moisture, over which the rising sun fell with sparkling and genial warmth. Every spire of grass bent as if with the weight of a diamond at its point. The vines and creeping shrubs that grew along the fences seemed blossoming with gems, so thick were the water-drops among their leaves; so bright were the sunbeams that kindled them into beauty. The atmosphere was full of cool, rich fragrance, and every gush of air, as it swept through the ponderous vehicle that bore Myra from her home, was delicious to breathe.

Ever and anon, as the stage followed the windings of the highway, Myra could obtain a view of her former home; silent stately, and refreshed, as it were, by the night storm, it rose before her tearful eyes. The proud old mansion, lifted on a terrace of hills above the level on which she traveled, could be seen for miles and miles around, and thus at every turn the noble features of all that she had given up were spread out before her gaze as if to mock her loneliness, or with their grandeur tempt her return.

But Myra scarcely thought of the stately old mansion. Her affectionate heart penetrated beyond its walls; she saw, as in a vision, one pale and gentle head asleep on its pillow, dreaming of scenes that would never be again. It was a memory of the slumbering household abandoned in its unconsciousness that filled the eyes of poor Myra with tears. She felt no regret for the noble property that she had rendered up without a sign. But the household links that she had broken still quivered about her heart, and Myra, as she cast her eyes back on her stately old home, could not choose but weep.

Our young traveler found her friends at New Castle willing to aid her, as the generous girls in Wilmington had been. It was arranged that an old gentleman, father of the lady whose roof had given shelter to the young girl, should proceed with her to Baltimore, and with this most unexceptionable escort Myra set forth. With the gentleman whose house she had left, she intrusted a note which was to be delivered to Mr. Whitney, should he by chance have taken passage in the boat expected in a few hours from Baltimore.

Anxious, hurried, and half ill with excitement, Myra and her companion reached Baltimore just in time to learn that a gentleman bearing the name of Whitney had taken passage in a boat which had passed them on their way.

Agitated by fresh fears, and wild with dread that the meeting between her father and her loved might take place in spite of all her efforts, the poor girl had no resource but to return with her companion, in the wild hope that her note might reach Mr. Whitney at New Castle, and thus prevent his proceeding on his route. By the return boat they reached the home of their generous friends once more, and there to her astonishment and dismay Myra found that a person of like name, but not the Mr. Whitney whom she sought to preserve from periling his life, had passed through New Castle.

It was now beyond the day appointed for her lover's arrival, and, without any knowledge of the time when he would pass through Baltimore, Myra had no better means of meeting him on the way than by remaining quietly with her friends till he should reach New Castle. The kind clergyman, who had so kindly given his protection to the adventurous girl, arranged that a strict watch should be kept at the landing. Thus day after day passed by, during which poor Myra suffered all the irksome pains of suspense, hoping, yet dreading the appearance of her lover, and haunted with a fear that her incensed parent might find out her place of shelter, and thus render all her efforts to prevent mischief to no avail. But thus harassed and worn out, she had only one resource. To wait—wait. To a nature ardent and impetuous as hers, this was a weary trial. So long as she had any thing to do, the excitement of action kept up her courage, but this life of inactive expectation wore upon her nerves, and she began to droop like a bird fettered in its cage. Thus she had lingered three days, imprisoned by her own free will, in the solitude of her chamber, when the event which she had most feared brought new agitation to her already overtaxed spirit. After days of vain and anxious search her parents had found out the place of her retreat.

It often happens that persons of strong and powerful organization become the slaves of their own will, and act in opposition to their best feelings and cool judgment, merely because that will has been expressed. Pride, stern, commanding pride, such as must have been the characteristic of a man like Mr. D., shrinks from the confession of fallibility, which a change of purpose too surely acknowledges. Imperious from nature and from that right of command which is so readily yielded to the rich even in our republican country, he had expressed his dislike and opposition to Mr. Whitney, and maintained it, not that he believed his suspicions of unworthiness just, but because they had been once expressed; and he, though generous, noble, affectionate, and filled with love for his adopted child, was the slave of his own will—that which he had said must be.

Upon the night of the storm this man had walked hours upon the veranda in front of his house, with the thunder booming and clashing overhead, and with the fierce lightning glaring across his pale face—and why? Not that he did not feel his heart tremble with every roar of the thunder, not that each blaze of lightning did not take away his breath. He was afraid of lightning, and for that very reason chose to brave it. Even the fear that was constitutional, that had grown and strengthened with him from childhood must yield to his will.

After that night of storm, when the strong man had wrestled with his better feelings as he had wrestled with his fear, to conquer both, he awoke to find his daughter gone. Like the lightning, she had disappeared, leaving him nothing to contend against. At first he would not believe the truth; even the wild anguish of his wife, who had lost her child, and refused to be comforted, seemed groundless. He would not believe in the effect of his own violence; but when the day passed by, when messenger after messenger returned, bearing no tidings of his daughter, the anguish which he endured could no longer be held under control. Strong as his pride of authority, deep and earnest as his nature, was his love for the young girl just driven from beneath his roof. Why had she been forced to go? Even to his own heart he could give no answer, save that he had willed her to love according to his wishes, and found her unable to wrestle with her affections as he had wrestled with the lightning. And now all the injustice of this obstinate adhesion to his own will became palpable to him, as it had long been to those who had suffered by it. With the impulse of a heart really capable of great magnanimity, he longed to make reparation to his child. The half of his great possessions he would have given for the privilege of holding her once more to his bosom, without the painful necessity of explanation. But a sleepless night was again followed by search and disappointment. It was strange how lonely and desolate that spacious house seemed when Myra was away. He missed the silvery ring of her laugh as he passed from room to room. Her empty seat at the table seemed to reproach him. He missed her light tread at night when she no longer came like a child, as she still was at heart, to ask for the good-night kiss. The tears and pale sorrow of his wife distressed him more keenly even than the void which Myra had left in that lordly dwelling. Altogether it was a mournful family—mournful as if a funeral had just passed from its midst.

Thus day followed day, and at length the suspense, which had become terrible to bear, was relieved: Myra's retreat at New Castle was made known to Mr. D.

It seems a matter of astonishment that high-minded and strong men should so often become dupes and victims to persons every way inferior, intellectually and morally; but when we reflect that the wise and generous are not only incapable of the low cunning and low motives which belong to the low of heart and mind, we can not marvel so much that they are incapable, also, of believing in the existence of these things, and that from an unbelief in evil, leave themselves unguarded to the insidious meanness they can not recognize as a portion of humanity.

We have said that in the house of Mr. D. there was a relative and guest to whom the departure of Myra from her home opened hopes of influence and ultimate gain, which were strong enough to arouse all the cupidity of his nature. This man had, with insidious meekness, reanimated the disquiet of the household, and with his soft words and silky manner, poured oil on the wrath of Mr. D., when he saw it yielding to the generous dictates of affection. He had excited the fears which drove Myra from her home, through the soft duplicity of his wife, and now it was his great desire to prevent an interview, or the least chance of reconciliation between the young girl and her parents. This man had found little difficulty in tracing Myra from the first, but his knowledge was kept secret until he found that Mr. D. was certain to hear of her movements from other sources; then openly claimed the merit of great exertions in finding out her place of shelter and volunteered, with the most disinterested air imaginable his influence in persuading the young girl to return home.

Glad to save himself the humiliation and pain of entreaties, from which his proud nature revolted, Mr. D. was well pleased to accept the friendly offer, and it was this man's arrival at New Castle, that startled Myra from the little repose she had been enabled to obtain. Mr. D. had authorized his messenger to induce Myra's return by gentle persuasion, by frank and generous promises that all should be forgiven, all forgotten. He made no stipulation, no reserve. All that he desired was the love and confidence of his child. To this was added many an affectionate message from the mother, whom Myra loved so fondly, and these were more than enough to have won the warm-hearted girl back to the bosom of her family.

Myra saw this man, and he gave Mr. D's message faithfully, even the caressing words of Mrs. D. were not withheld; but when he saw tears swell up and fill the fine eyes which Myra turned upon him as he gave the message—when he saw a gush of passionate tenderness sweep across her face, the man changed gradually in his manner. His eye, his downcast look, the compression of his mouth, all told that something had been kept back. He seemed struggling with himself, and Myra saw that all was not as it should be. The young girl had no doubt of this man's sincerity—she had always believed him to be her friend. How then was she to reconcile this restless manner, this sort of caution that gleamed in his eyes and spoke in every feature of his face, with the frank message of which he was the bearer?

After much anxious questioning the man consented to speak, but it was only out of the deepest and most self-sacrificing friendship to her. It was periling the favor of Mr. D. forever, but still he would speak. He would not urge a creature so young and lovely to rush blindfold into the power of a man exasperated as Mr. D. was against her. True, all these promises had been sent; but in reality, the hate of her father had only been aggravated against Mr. Whitney by her flight. Mr. D. was implacable as ever, and instead of receiving his child with kindness, his sole desire was to win her by false protestations into his power again, and then punish her with all his haughty strength.

All this was repeated with the most perfect appearance of sincerity. The truth seemed to have been wrested from this man's heart, only by the solemn obligations of friendship. Myra was very grateful for this friendly warning, and the traitor left her strengthened in her purpose, but with an aching and desolate heart.

Not an hour after this interview, Mr. Whitney arrived at New Castle. Various reasons for delay had kept him behind his appointment, but Myra's agent had been vigilant, and her note reached him as he left the boat. He came directly to the residence of her friend, ignorant of all that had transpired to drive Myra from the protection of her own home.

Mr. Whitney had left the young girl gay, blooming, and brilliant, with joyous anticipations—she met him now pale and drooping, her eyes heavy with tears, her form swayed by the weight of her grief, like the stalk of a flower on which the dew has fallen too heavily.

"And now," he said, when she had told him all, "there is but one course for us to pursue, and that, thank Heaven, is one to secure our happiness. This man is not your father, and has no legal authority over you. I will not speak of his injustice to me—of his harshness to you—for in former years I know that he has been kind."

Myra's eyes filled with grateful tears. There was something in this gentle forbearance that touched her deeply.

"Let us be united now, Myra; no one has authority over you. I am, in all things, independent!"

It was hard to resist that pleading voice, those eyes so full of hopeful tenderness, but Myra drew away her hand with an air of gentle dignity, and a painful smile parted her lips.

"No," she said, "no; I am here of my own will, unsolicited, unexpected. It must not be said that your wife ran away from her father's roof only to be married."

The proud delicacy with which this was spoken—so earnest in its simplicity—left no room for a doubt. Mr. Whitney did not plead with her, though greatly disappointed; he merely took her hand, with a smile, and said:

"But this seems like rejecting me altogether. Surely there is too much of pride here. Would you suffer thus to save a life, and then render that life valueless, Myra?"

The color came and went upon Myra's pale cheek. Now that he was by her side, her hand in his, those eyes upon her face, the poor girl felt how impossible it was to part from him forever.

"I have friends—relatives in the West Indies," she said. "Let me go to them. Come to me there, with the frank and full consent of your parents to our union, and I will be your wife."

"No, not there, not so far. In Philadelphia—let me place you under the protection of your friends there. I will visit my parents—their presence and full consent shall sanction our marriage. Will not this arrangement satisfy even your delicacy, beloved?"

Again the warm rose tinge came and went on Myra's cheek, and the tears that still swam in her eyes grew bright as diamonds with the smile that broke through them.

"Yes," she said, "this is enough."

Three hours from that time Myra and her lover were on their way to Philadelphia, but the good clergyman and his wife went with them from New Castle, and left their sweet charge with her friends, while Mr. Whitney proceeded to the home of his parents.

And now, when the necessity for resistance was gone, the reaction of all this wild excitement swept over and prostrated her. Like a plant that keeps green so long as the frost is in its leaves, but withers and droops with the first glow of sunshine, her strength gave way, and there was a time when her very life seemed in jeopardy.

Thus weak and feeble, poor Myra lay upon her couch in the quiet gloom of her sick-chamber, and shrinking from the slightest sound, with that sensitive dread which was itself a pain, she heard a noise upon the stairs. It seemed like the hesitating tread of a man, blended with the eager and suppressed remonstrance of some person who desired to check his progress. Myra began to tremble, for even this was enough to shake every nerve of her slight frame. She lifted her pale hand, put back the tresses from her temple, and made a faint effort to lift her head from the pillow, but in vain.

"My child—my child refuse to see her father? I will not believe it!"

"Father! father!" broke from the lips of that pale girl, and she sank on her pillow gasping for breath.

All was hushed then, the door opened softly, and through the gloom which hung around her couch, Myra saw the stately form of the old man who had so long been her father. His face was pale, and tears stood upon his cheek, as he bent down and kissed her forehead. Myra smiled, and drawing a deep breath closed her eyes, and then opened them with a look of touching love.

"Father!"

"My child!"

The old man sat down with her hand in his, and began smoothing the slender fingers with his other palm, as he had done so often in her childhood. This little act brought a world of pleasant old memories back to Myra's heart, one after another, like drops of cool dew upon a half-blighted flower. She turned gently, and placed her other hand in the old man's palm.

He bent down and kissed the two little hands he clasped in his.

"And mamma!" whispered Myra.

"Your mamma has been pining for her child, Myra, and I am here to take you home again."

"But you hate him—you—you—" The poor girl broke off with a shudder.

"No, I will like him for your sake, love!" was the kind reply.

Myra closed her eyes, and tears broke through the dark lashes.

The old man now smiled, as he saw the tremulous joy his words had brought to that pale face.

"We will have the wedding at D. Place, and when you go away again, Myra, it must not be without a blessing."

"Oh, papa, I am so happy," whispered the poor girl, drawing a deep breath. She did not unclose her eyes again, but a sweet placidity stole over her face, and she fell into a calm sleep, the first that had visited her eyelids in many a long day and night.

Never had D. Place looked more beautiful than it appeared on the day when Myra returned to it, with her happy father. The fine old building, with all its surrounding trees, was bathed in a flood of sunshine, that hung over the whole landscape like the mist of a bridal vail. The servants were all out to receive their young mistress as she alighted from the carriage; even the hunting dogs came whining and yelping from their kennels, riotous with joy, as so many politicians the day after an election. Myra had smiles for all; but as her eyes fell upon the gentle mother, who had loved her so devotedly, the young girl broke away, her cheeks glowing, her eyes full of tears, and threw herself into the arms that were joyously opened to receive her.

"Oh, mamma, I never expected to be so happy again!" she cried, shaking back her curls, and gazing upon the face of her mother with a look of thrilling affection. "But you are pale, mamma!"

"No, not now; but I am very, very happy, Myra."

"But I have only brought her home that she may leave us again," said Mr. D., with a frank smile, as his wife held out one hand to welcome him, while the other still clung to her child.

"I know, I know; but that is quite a different thing," answered the happy mother, drawing Myra into the house.

As Myra passed up to her old room she met the household traitor, who had so deliberately misrepresented his friend. The man held out his hand.

"No," said Myra, drawing back with quiet contempt. "For your children's sake I have not exposed your baseness, but there can be no friendship between us in future."

"So because your father has changed, I am to be censured for misrepresentation," answered the man with consummate self-possession. "But this is the usual reward of an honest endeavor to serve."

Myra passed on, without reply.

Mr. D. was not a man to make partial atonement for an error. A prompt and urgent request was forwarded to Mr. Whitney and his parents, that they should make D. Place, and not Philadelphia, the destination of their journey. Meantime every arrangement was commenced for the wedding, and thus Myra's path of life lay among blossoms and in the sunshine again. It was a pleasant thing to wait then, for a world of happiness seemed dawning for her in the future.

Mr. Whitney came at last, and with him the revered parent, whose consent to his son's marriage had been frankly given. After all their trials and adventures, the young couple were to be married quietly at last under the shelter of home, surrounded by those who knew and loved them best.

You should have seen Myra Clark as she came down the massive staircase in her bridal dress that wedding-night. Her *petite* figure, graceful as a sylph, was rendered still more ethereal by the misty floating of her bridal vail. The fragrance of a few white blossoms floated through her ringlets, and her small foot, clad in its slipper of snowy satin, scarcely seemed to touch the stairs as she descended.

Whitney stood by the open door ready to receive his bride. With her own peculiar and feminine grace she met him; the glow upon her cheek took a deeper rose-tint as she laid her small hand in his. She trembled a little, just enough to give a flower-like tremor to the folds of her vail, and for one instant the shadow of deep thought swept over her face.

The bridegroom was very tall, and this gave to Myra a look still more feminine and child-like, as she stood by his side.

"Are you ready, dearest?" he said, bending gently over her.

She gave a faint start, and lifted her large brown eyes to his with a smile of such deep love and holy trust, as seldom looks up from a soul merely human. That smile was answer enough. The next moment they stood within the broad light that flooded the drawing-room. A few words—a few murmured blessings—perchance a few tears—for the tears of affectionate regret are sometimes the brightest jewels that can be cast at the feet of a bride—and then Myra Clark became a wife.

CHAPTER EIGHT

A DISCOVERY

Pain! pain! art thou wrestling here with man,
For the broken gold of the wasted span?
Art thou straining thy rock on his tortured nerve,
Till his firmest hopes from their anchor swerve,
Till the burning tears from his eyeballs flow,
And his manhood yields a cry of woe?

Death! death! do I see thee with weapon dread—
Art thou laying thy hand on his noble head?
Lo! the wife is here, with her sleepless eye,
To dispute each step of thy victory.
She doth fold that form in her soul's embrace,
And her prayer swells high from its resting-place.

In a quiet village of New York, Myra Whitney made her home with the man who had won her against so much opposition and amid so many trials. She had cast off the splendor of her old life, and, sharing the fortunes of her husband, began a new and still more noble existence; but directly came one to the little Eden with news that would henceforth and forever more drive quiet away from her home.

A man who was well acquainted with the frauds that had been practiced on the infant heiress, sought out the young bride and told her of the vast wealth illegally withheld from her by the executors of Daniel Clark's estate—told her of that which stirred the proud blood in her veins more warmly than any idea of wealth could have done—the doubt that had been craftily thrown on her own legitimacy, and thus on the fair fame of her mother.

From that day all hope of repose fled from her happy home. A stern duty was before her—that of retrieving the wrongs heaped on her mother, and of wresting the honorable name of a father, whom she worshiped even in his memory, from the odium that had been fastened upon his actions. Joined to all this, was the natural ambition of a high-spirited and proud young woman to claim her true position in the world, and to endow the man of her choice with wealth justly her own, but of which he had been all unconscious at the time of their marriage; and now commenced that stern strife between justice and fraud which has for more than twenty years made the romance of our courts. With her young husband Myra went to New Orleans, and there gathered up those threads of evidence which laid the iniquity, which had darkened her whole life, bare before the world. There she found Madame De Gordette, her mother, the Zulima of our true story, and there, for the first time, she learned all the domestic romance of her own history: the anguish that had followed her mother, the remorse and solemn restitution that had marked the closing hours of her father's life.

To a being ambitious and imaginative as Myra, this interview with her mother was calculated to make a painful and solemn impression. The one great idea of her life became a firm resolve; to that she was ready to sacrifice domestic peace and all those feminine aims which spring from highly cultivated tastes. Still womanly in all her acts, she took upon herself the research and duties of a man, not alone, but hand in hand with the husband whose happiness and aggrandizement would be secured by these exertions.

But the vast property of Daniel Clark had been scattered far and wide by the men who had taken it in trust. The personal property had melted away first, then tract after tract of land, block upon block of real estate had followed, till the claimants, most of them innocent purchasers, might be counted by hundreds. But the greater the obstacles that presented themselves, the more resolute became this young creature in the advocacy of her own just cause. All necessary evidence of the existence of a last will and of its destruction was secured; witnesses of Zulima's marriage with Daniel Clark in Philadelphia still existed. The mother herself, though shrinking from the cruel publicity of her wrongs, gave such aid as her naturally shrinking nature, now rendered almost timid by suffering, would permit. Men of influence, struck by the sublime spectacle of a fair young creature, with scarcely the physical strength of a child, entering courageously on a battle where such fearful odds prevailed against her, came generously to her support. The great fight of her life opened hopefully; victory might be distant, but she would not doubt that it would come at last.

But in the midst of her first struggle she had forgotten to be prudent, indeed precaution was scarcely natural to that early period of her life. By adoption she had become a child of the North, but the warm genial glow of her blood still sympathized with the sunny climate to which she had moved, fearlessly, with her little children at the most dangerous season of the year.

But her husband was a northern man by birth, and he did not assimilate readily to the hot, moist climate of New Orleans. The excitement into which he was thrown doubtless added to the causes which oppressed him; in the midst of his struggles in the full bloom and force of his manly youth, Whitney was stricken down among the first victims that the yellow fever seized upon that year.

They were living at a hotel in the heart of the city, with no home comforts around them, and surrounded by a crowd of enemies—such as spring from hotly-contested law-suits where many persons are interested in the defense. To all those persons who had in any way attained a claim on the property of Daniel Clark, his daughter was, of course, held as an aggressive enemy—a woman who had come with her ambition and her doubtful claims to disturb the tranquillity of a great city. Many of these persons, having bought the property they possessed in good faith, really felt her action to be a great wrong—they had no means of knowing the facts of a case over which so many legal minds have struggled, and naturally sided with their own visible interests against the fair claimant. Thus the yellow fever that struck her husband down in a single hour, found Myra in the midst of enemies such as few women have ever encountered.

All day Myra had been lonely and sad, her children felt the heavy effects of the climate, and her own bright energies seemed yielding themselves to the enervating influences that surrounded them. Sometimes in the great struggle that she had commenced so bravely, Myra felt the painful reaction which springs from a long strain upon the energies. That day she had been thinking of her pretty home in the North, of its quietude, its cool thickets, and the great forest-trees that overshadowed it. Near the house was a spring of water—one of those natural outgushes of crystal waves which children love to play near, and whose flow is remembered as the sweetest music in the world afterward. In the heat and closeness of her room, Myra's thoughts had been constantly going back to this spring. The children also had prattled about it between themselves, and once had joined in a pretty petition to the languid mother that they might go back again and play out-of-doors.

Myra felt the tears come to her eyes as she answered them; there was no real cause for this depression, but it had fallen heavily upon her all day; she felt like snatching up her little ones and fleeing with them to the northward, where they might all breathe and laugh freely.

While the young wife was in this strange mood, the door opened and her husband came in. She glanced up in his face smiling a welcome, but his eyes were heavy, and a hot crimson burning on either cheek startled her.

She put the children aside, and seizing his hand gave another terrified look in his face. He tried to smile, but instantly lifted a hand to his forehead and groaned aloud.

"What is this, my husband—are you ill, or have you been walking in the hot sun?"

He withdrew his hot hand from her clasp, and sharply ordered the children back as they came laughing toward him. The little ones began to cry, but Myra would not be repulsed, she was no child to shrink away from a sharp word, though it was the first she had ever known him give her darlings.

"Ah! now I am sure you must be ill," she said, hushing the children. "Who ever saw you cross before, my Whitney, above all things, to them?"

"They must not come near me—send them away, and go yourself," he said, huskily.

"What! I—I go away?" cried the young wife, with a groan of indignation breaking up through her terror. "What can you think of me, Whitney?"

"For their sake—for your own, Myra," he said, pushing her away. "Child—child, it is the fever that is upon me."

She looked at him eagerly, almost wildly; her pale lips fell apart and her cheek grew cold as snow.

"Take the children away," she said, motioning backward with her hand to a mulatto girl who stood looking on. "Take them quite away into your own room, Agnes, and be still."

The little ones went reluctantly and with tears standing in their wild eyes. It was so strange for them to be sent away when papa came in—then he looked so odd and stood so unsteadily on the floor; besides mamma was beginning to cry—they would go back and ask her what it was all about.

But no, the firm little maid held them tight and forced them, struggling, through the door. She knew what those symptoms foreboded, and a sudden dread seized upon her. Yes, she would save the little ones—that was all she could hope for—and away she dragged them into her own little room which was distant from the infected chamber.

Myra forgot her children, forgot every thing in the frightful symptoms that burned on her husband's face, and shot fire in to the hands she clasped and wrung in her own.

"O husband! my husband, it is not that—not the fever, God help us! You have been in the heat—you are tired out; a glass of ice-water and a little rest will drive this headache away."

"Oh, it is terrible, Myra, my temples seem splitting with the pain," he murmured, holding his head between both hands and reeling to and fro.

"But it is the heat—it is the heat!" she persisted, determined to believe herself.

"It is death!—O Myra! I fear it is death!"

She began to tremble in all her limbs, a wild terror broke into her brown eyes, giving them an unearthly brightness.

"Oh, don't—don't! the bare idea kills me," she pleaded, flinging her arms around him.

He struggled and tried to force her away, but the fire of disease and the power of her great love was stronger than his confused will. She drew him toward the bed and forced him down to the pillows, praying him to be quiet and to try to sleep.

While he lay moaning on the pillows, she ran for ice-water and gave it to his hot lips, bound his forehead with wet napkins, and strove, in her sweet feminine way, to assuage the pain which had seized so fiercely upon him. To have seen that slight creature acting as a nurse to the being she most loved, you would hardly have believed it possible that she possessed sufficient energy to take a controlling lead in one of the most important law-cases that ever astonished our country—that she had breasted difficulties and outlived discouragements, before which strong men might have retreated, without a forfeiture of courage. In that sick-room she was gentle as childhood, but quick as lightning to seize upon any means of mitigating the pain that held that young man as in the embrace of a fiend.

Hour after hour she watched in that sick-chamber. The doctor came, ordered the usual remedies, and went away again, with a heart that felt little and a face that told nothing at all. His course of practice was unvaried—the same medicines in almost every case—copious bleeding; vague, wild hopes in the loving hearts that ached around the bed; then the last fatal symptom and death—thus it went day after day.

Poor Myra! How she searched that man's leaden eyes for some little gleam of hope when he came into that sick-chamber! How eagerly she strove to read features that never changed to a thought or a feeling, even when death stood close by! Still she would not despair; had not every obstacle given way to the force of her own will so far in her life—was she to be baffled and conquered now? To her warm heart it seemed impossible that death could strike a form so full of manly strength, or that she could live an hour after him if the great calamity did come.

Alas! with all her experience and force, Myra was yet to learn how difficult it is for a human heart to break of grief, or exhaust itself with trouble. If a wish to die could induce the dark destroyer to strike, many a breathing—nay, blooming form would be lying low, which is now doomed to run its course to the end.

One day, it was less than a week after the first attack, Myra was called to the bedside of her husband. A great and terrible change had come upon that splendid form. The flesh had seemed to melt away from his limbs like mist from the uplands; his eyes were hollow; the skin upon his forehead was yellowish brown.

"Myra, my poor wife."

She bent down and kissed the fever-stained forehead.

"My husband! You are better; there, the brightness is coming back to your eyes."

"No, Myra, no; I feel strangely but not better."

A movement of impotent sorrow revealed the struggle with which the poor woman strove to disprove this truth to her heart.

"Don't say that—you don't understand. Wait till the doctor comes, he will tell you that I am right."

The sick man moved his hand feebly on the pillow, and a moan broke from his lips.

Just then the doctor came in from his rounds in the infested city. The young wife appealed to him, with her mournful eyes trembling with an awful dread as his fingers touched the pulse.

"O doctor! Is he better?"

"Yes, undoubtedly."

Myra burst into tears; the invalid brightened a little, then turned his face on the pillow, and great tears rolled down his cheeks.

"No, doctor," he murmured, "no!"

"It is my opinion we have every thing to hope here, madam. Let us take a little more blood, and all will go on well."

Bandages were brought; the sharp lancet bit its way a third time into those hot veins, and directly a servant bore out a great white toilet-bowl frothing over with the red life drawn from a frame already exhausted with its battle against the fever.

"There, madam," said the doctor, laying the wounded arm of his patient tenderly on the counterpane. "He will do well now, have no fear; I will drop in this evening; follow old directions and keep him quiet."

"O doctor! I can not speak my thankfulness, my heart is so full."

"There is no necessity of words," said the doctor, complacently; "or for gratitude either, so far as I am concerned."

Myra followed the man, whom she looked upon as something more than human, into the hall.

"Ah, doctor, are you sure that he is better—is was not done to cheer him up?" she cried, while her poor lips began to quiver with the fear that crept over her.

"Nothing of the sort, dear lady. He is doing well enough; but take care of yourself."

Myra smiled on him through her tears. "God bless you for this comfort," she said leaning over the baluster.

After he was gone, Myra ran into the room where her children were kept safe from contagion, and gathering them to her bosom, lavished rapturous caresses on their smiling faces.

"He is better—he is better, my darlings; he, your blessed, blessed papa. Kiss me a thousand times, and when I am gone go down on your knees so, with these angel faces lifted to heaven, and thank God—do you understand, children?—thank God, that papa is better and will live."

The children obeyed her, and dropping on their knees, lifted their pretty faces heavenward, like the cherubs we see in Raphael's pictures, looking the prayers they had no language to utter.

Then Myra, having subdued her great joy, went back to the sickroom again. How still and deathly he lay under the white cloud of sunshine that brooded over the bed! Myra held her breath, and listened for some sign of improvement. His eyes were closed, and his lips shrunk together and closed motionless in their golden pallor. How the heart of that fond woman cheated itself. His languid stillness was a good sign to her.

"Yes," she whispered, sitting down by the bed, and softly clasping his feeble hand. "There is no pain now; he rests sweetly."

He heard her and clasped her fingers with feeble recognition, but did not speak or attempt to utter a word. Still the great tears rolled down his face, and she knew he was conscious.

Thus two or three hours passed and then the fever grew rampant again, and fell upon that weak form like a vampyre, drinking up all the life that the lancet had left. Myra began to be frightened, and hoped impatiently for the doctor to come. There was something in the case that she could not understand; doubtless, it was all right, but the look of that haggard face was appalling.

At last the physician came slowly, and with that slow method which is so irksome to an impatient heart. He came to the bed, felt of the patient's pulse, laid the hand gently down, and turned away muttering that she might go on as before, there were no fresh directions to give.

Now the patient opened his eyes, and fixed them with mournful reproach on the doctor's face; he did not attempt to speak, but the great tears gathered slowly in his eyes, and the dark lashes closed again.

As usual Myra followed the doctor out of the room.

"Tell me," she said, "he is no worse—he is getting well; there is no danger now."

The doctor drew on his glove, smoothing it to the hand, while she was speaking.

"There is no hope, my dear madam; not a gleam. He must die before morning; did you not observe the black on his lips."

"Die before morning—my husband. Oh, no! You want to see if I have all the courage people talk about; but you see, doctor, I am a poor little coward. One does not fight with death. Don't you see how I tremble? Don't, don't carry this any further. I'm not very strong, and—and—oh, my God! my God! why don't you speak to me?"

"Indeed, my poor lady, I have nothing more to say; it would give me great satisfaction to give you hope if I had any myself. But the last fatal symptom has come, no skill on earth can save him; it is but a question of time now—hardly that, in fact."

The doctor was going down-stairs as he spoke, for he would gladly have avoided the anguish that came like a storm into that white face, but Myra sprang after him, seizing hold of his arm.

"O doctor! O doctor!" she cried, gasping for breath, "is this true?"

"Indeed, I regret to say it, but nothing could be more certain."

Her hand dropped from his arm, her whole being grew cold till the icy chill penetrated to her heart. She watched him, as he glided down the stairs, with a strained and wild look. Then she turned and went in to the chamber where her husband lay dying.

When Myra came forth again she was a widow. In one of those cemeteries hemmed in by moss-grown walls and filled with gloomy verdure, they laid the young husband down to his long rest. A pale little woman with two fair children wondering at their black crape dresses, stood by silent and filled with a dreary wonder that it took so little time to render a human life desolate. There was no noisy grief in that solemn inclosure; the little children held their breath in vague awe. The mother looked on as if those strange men were burying her heart which she could never rescue back from the grave.

Years went by—life made its inevitable claims, and the great battle of the law went on, which Myra fought out in behalf of the parents who were dead and the children of her husband. In the course of this struggle, a brave old man, one who had served his country well and stood at the head of its armies, laid his heart and his well-earned fame at Myra's feet, and she became his wife. A few years and he, in the very city which had proved so fatal to her first love, lay down amid his ripe honors, and died, blessing her with his last word on earth. And now she still—indomitable still—untiring fights the great battle alone, and another year will prove that the life-struggle of Myra Clark Gaines has not been without its victory, and that energy, even in a delicate woman, can at last overtake justice.

THE END.

THE HISTORY BEHIND THE NOVEL

Ann Stephens' *Myra, The Child of Adoption* was inspired by the true story of Myra Clark Gaines. Mrs. General Edmund Gaines was the key figure in the country's longest-running legal case and perhaps the most sensational case of the nineteenth century.

In 1830, twenty-five-year-old Myra learned she had been adopted and that her natural father, Daniel Clark, was a multimillionaire merchant from New Orleans. Myra's fight to claim her birthright and establish herself as the legal heir to Clark's fortune spanned more than fifty years.

"The Great Gaines Case," as it became known, had all the elements of scandal and intrigue that make good front-page newspaper copy. According to Clark's will, drafted in 1811, upon his death his mother was to be awarded his estate. Myra insisted her father had drafted a second will—two months prior to his death in 1813—that acknowledged her existence and named her as sole beneficiary. She accused the executioners of the 1811 will of destroying the later document.

The legal squabbling was made public on a daily basis. Myra's name became one of the most recognizable in the United States. She capitalized on her popularity, outlining the horrors of war on a speaking

Myra Clark Gaines

tour. Her lectures were well attended, but mostly by curious citizens interested in the progress of the case involving her inheritance.

"The Great Gaines Case" was never fully resolved while Myra was alive. The court's determination that she was indeed the legal heir was overturned numerous times. The case was still being tried when Myra died in 1885. When the case was settled in 1891, the $35 million estate had been reduced to a mere $100,000 due to lawyer fees and other debts.

The story of Myra Clark Gaines' long struggle to remove the stain of illegitimacy associated with her name and take possession of what she believed was rightfully hers has been the focus of many short stories and novels. The most-read narrative remains Ann Stephens' romantic version of the tale.

SUGGESTED READING

American Women's Dime Novel Project, George Mason University, http://chnm.gmu.edu/dimenovels/.

Cox, Randolf. *The Dime Novel Companion*. Greenwood Press, Westport, Conn., 2000.

Johannsen, Albert. *The House of Beadle and Adams and Its Nickel and Dime Novels; The Story of a Vanished Literature*. The University of Oklahoma Press, Norman, Okla., 1950.

———. *The House of Beadle and Adams and Its Nickel and Dime Novels; The Story of a Vanished Literature*, supplement edition. The University of Oklahoma Press, Norman, Okla., 1962.

Sullivan, Larry E., and Lydia Shuman. *Pioneers, Passionate Ladies, and Private Eyes: Dime Novels, Series Books & Paperbacks*. Haworth Press, Binghamton, N.Y., 1996.